Slipstream

Book 1 of
The Slipstream series

Alice Godwin

SLIPSTREAM

Book 1 in *The Slipstream* series.

The moral rights of Alice Godwin to be identified as the author of this work have been asserted.

Copyright 2022

Hague Publishing

PO Box 451

Bassendean, Western AUSTRALIA 6934

Email: contact@haguepublishing.com

Web: www.haguepublishing.com

ISBN 978-0-6488346-8-7

Cover: Slipstream by Jade Zivanovic

http://www.steampowerstudios.com.au/

Typeset Garamond 12/13

Dedication

To my family ~
past, present & future,
human & non human,
in this universe, or another –
& Mars.

SLIPSTREAM

A red rose absorbs all colours but red;

red is therefore the one colour it is not.

Aleister Crowley.

Chapter One

Like two doomed ships that pass in storm
We had crossed each other's way:
But we made no sign, we said no word . . .

Oscar Wilde

The Past

The sky was azure blue, although Jo knew the pollution levels were extremely high today. Perhaps the toxins actually made the blueness of the sky deeper, richer: cobalt blue, heavy metal cyan, cerulean chemical contamination. What colour was quicksilver poisoning?

Blue, most probably, she thought.

Our veins contain blood that looks blue, not the red oxygenated blood of the arteries but a tired, depleted poison. Yet blood is always red, even death-blood, soaking out like some sad, dark stain.

I've never come across a corpse that leaked blue blood, but there is a first time for everything, she mused.

Jo slipped on her glasses of polarised black that turned everything into underwater murk, a place of shadows and slid into her ecopod. The streets above were narrow and harrowing; she gratefully left the outer world and went underground where the freeways broadened out into cobwebs of steel and asphalt. Here she could drive for days and not even have to surface for air. She headed west; following the curve of the river as it wound its way above, silently brimming with its own deep thoughts. She resurfaced three hours later; the plains were dusty, dry. Awnings that doubled as solar ventilators shielded the apartments. Everything was grey or ochre; no vegetation grew on the outside, and the buildings faced inwards to their own private oasis. Perspex ceilings diffused the light, and the humidity was sweet and gentle. Stay, live, love, die in your own highly organic, pure environment.

Jo checked in with security and entered the rainforest. Parrots flew through the trees, vines grew and bloomed with flowers the size of small children, butterflies fluttered, and the air was misty. The low music was calming and watery; synthesised torrents flowing over emerald cliffs. She always felt slightly unnerved with all these subliminal aural pacifiers – they just left everyone so alpha-waved that talking to them was like speaking to angels on lithium.

I don't need this case, she thought as she crossed a bridge that swung perceptibly beneath her, woven using organic raffia fibres.

The apartment was located near a pond overgrown with lotus flowers; their narcotic scent was overpowering. Jo pressed her card into the slot and the wall moved. The place was dark: the walls, furniture, floors, and ceiling; everything was a dark serpentine metal. The floor was rough and of a serrated substance that reminded Jo of scaly creatures.

The body lay on the floor near a doorway. It was a woman: young, Asian, and pretty – once. She was naked – her full belly was slashed open, blood and gelatinous bits stained her skin, and the floor around her. A carnal slaughterhouse smell pervaded the room; white-coated professionals slinked around like lions circling a potential meal.

Jo entered another room. Connor sat at the kitchen bar drinking caffeine and smoking.

He's so fucking ugly, she thought.

It always struck her that way. Although she had known him for years, his outward appearance still surprised her. He was a child's nightmare – a monster, a hideous beast. Yet condemned to eternal loneliness. But his eyes were nice – that always struck her too; soft and sorrowful.

"What am I here for?" she asked bluntly, staring into those sad eyes.

He passed over a forensic plastic bag containing a piece of flat crystal. Paper-thin, etched with markings – a five-pointed star within a circle within a cross within a flaming comet; the sign of the Rapturists.

"Haven't seen one of these for a while," she said wistfully.

"That's why you're here." He smiled, and his monster face looked even more grotesque and gargoyle-like.

I could fall in love with him, she thought, if I wasn't the logical realist I am.

"The Rapturists were part of that profusion of end-time, plague-time cults." Jo said. "They're long gone, or at the very least diluted into nothing."

"It was found on the body. A calling card perhaps."

"A decoy."

"You saw the body, the stomach?"

Jo nodded.

"Nearly full term. They just yanked it out, took it with them, and left her to bleed to death." His voice was edged with bitterness. Connor rarely let any emotion creep into his persona; something had really gotten to him.

"What haven't you told me?" she asked.

"Haven't lost your touch, have you?"

"Not yet," she said too brightly. He reached into his pocket and pulled out another bag, another crystal. This one was high-tech, hologram etched, shining with multi-fractured laser lights, very expensive.

"She was wearing this around her neck," he said as he passed it over. "We scanned it. It's basically a highly evolved amulet. Protects the wearer from evil. It's superb quality and not cheap, but the rich have their superstitions too. The signature is unusual, an eccentric engraver, he made very few of these, none were ever sold, all were gifts. He was a founding member of the Pacific Rim Rapturists and he died fifteen years ago. She was his daughter."

"Connor, like I said we're talking years ago. Sects of that nature don't hang around, they evolve, change, metamorphose into something else. Apocalyptic visions are not the order anymore."

"Things like this don't die, Jo. They just go underground – become secretive; more dangerous."

Jo stood and stretched. She ran her fingers through her short, blonde hair. "You think because of my background, I can find things others won't."

"I think, Jo, you have the ability to just about find anything."

Chapter Two

The Present

Raven squinted in the strong afternoon sun; she looked at the derelict buildings, the weeds sprouting up among the broken bricks, the rows of windows each shattered in an almost uniform jaggedness, the sun-bleached lettering advertising something long forgotten. The bars at the window mockingly protecting decay and dust. For the first time, Raven felt uneasy. The sun was scorching as it beat down on her shoulders, her mouth was dry, and she felt nervous and skittish.

She lit a cigarette; she had swapped a small but extremely warm blanket for it from one of the transients passing through her home. She threw the match on the ground. The grass around her boots crackled with aridness and she hastily kicked soil over the match. An overwhelming dread of fire set her heart beating; she could almost see the flames igniting the dry vegetation, becoming an inferno. She imagined the flames licking up the paintwork, buckling the bars, melting the shards of glass so that they ran down the brickwork like tears. She could almost hear the screams, awful, terrifying.

But the dead don't scream, she thought. Only the living scream.

She felt the smoke glide down inside her throat, and her body react to the stimulating effects of the chemicals. Most of them were now outlawed, but contraband was always there if you knew where to find it.

The inside of the crumbling warehouse was exactly as Raven remembered; quiet and undisturbed. Above her, light chains wavered in the breeze; metallic vines grew from the roof, trying in vain to reach their brothers lying idle and dead below them. She came here to get away from the noise that was always around her. This was the only place where she couldn't hear the endless buzzing, the whisperings of the web, the electromagnetic humming that surrounded everything, everywhere. Here her head was silent. She made herself comfortable on a canvas shrouded mass and fell asleep.

***

It was the singing that stayed with her as she woke. It lingered faintly; so sweet and alluring that the world might just dissolve and become meaningless. It enthralled her. She could feel it working its sublime magic as it pulled her under again, as it had that first time she had heard it. There was a haunting, eerie tone to the singing, like she imagined the sirens might sound as they lured the sailors to the rocks. It tore into her mind, her heart, her soul. It beckoned her like a lover and as the nocturnal notes ebbed and flowed – she ebbed and flowed with it.

Long shadows blurred everything. She lay staring at the roof, at the cobwebbed girders, their ochre colour lost among the silver diaphanous gowns that clung to them. She tried to get up, but found she couldn't. Was she still dreaming? She reached for her phone. The screen was dark. No connection.

This is why you come here, so you can't go in. So you can get away, she reminded herself.

She closed her eyes and found herself falling, entering that free-fall state and then she was there, navigating the silver streams.

It was crystalline and tranquil; perfect is what it is. Perfect.

She sensed an echo, feeling the stream around her, flowing silently. It was beautiful; like an aurora, the colours vibrant, unearthly. Then she sensed it again more strongly; a heartbeat difference in the current. There were four of them, four riders in the slipstream – four where there should've been none. She stayed waiting, sensing their approach, watching the colours switch in acknowledgement of their presence, shifting to a darker spectrum. Closer and closer they came until there was only nano seconds between her and them. She saw their silhouettes, breaking up the stream like ripples on water, inky swirls, shadowy, indistinct.

She woke, heart pounding and sweat trickling down the side of her face. Above, a pale glowing orb moved from behind a cloud and streams of moonlight danced in spirals down through the skylights. The cobwebs glimmered with a phosphorescent glow, the light chains and the grimy machinery radiated sparkling moon dust. The place shone with a white lustre as though it were covered with a thin sprinkling of glittering ice.

Raven walked outside, and looked at her phone. The screen was still black. She looked around her, and tried not to focus too hard on all the shimmering shapes that had coalesced in this empty wasteland. She didn't want to see them clearly, especially one of them. It was too similar to what she had seen in the slipstream. And what was there, shouldn't be here.

Chapter Three

Drowning is not so pitiful as the attempt to rise.

Emily Dickinson

The mid-morning sun was bright and hot, and it edged around the curtains, determined to illuminate the space that it was denied. Its rays edged through the minuscule gaps in-between, and managed to lighten one corner and, then finding an ally in the mirror, bounced off the reflective surface finding more nooks and crannies to flare and dazzle out of. Halo sat up, cradled his head in his hands before running his fingers through his wavy black hair. He felt terrible – his head pounded like a drummer was running amok in an confined space, his eyes ached, and his mouth tasted like an old garbage can. He stumbled to the bathroom, and avoiding the light leaned against the shower tiles, turning the taps on, letting the hot water scald him into wakefulness.

The towel he reached for smelled musty and stale, so he threw it on the floor and padded naked and dripping into the kitchen, thankful that the blinds and curtains were tightly drawn. There, he searched the fridge for something, anything. Since the fridge contained virtually nothing, it was a search soon completed. He drank the last of the orange juice, refraining from reading the use by date just in case. Not that it would've meant anything, He had absolutely no idea what the date was, or even what day it was. He put the last of the ground coffee into the coffee machine and watched as it dripped into his mug.

Halo sat at the kitchen bar and looked around. The place looked unfamiliar, and he tried to remember the last time he had been in here. He couldn't. Days and weeks swam together in his mind like thousands of colourful fish in an overpopulated pond. The coffee revived him somewhat. He walked with it through the French doors and into a courtyard that was overgrown with banana palms and bamboo. It had originally been designed to have a Japanese feel to it and there was, almost hidden, a small pond complete with a bamboo server, a shishi-odoshi, that slowly filled up with water before pivoting downwards and tipping the water out with a splash. Bamboo chimes tinkled in the breeze. It was now altogether too unruly to be still considered Japanese, though it retained a darkly oriental feel to it like an old forgotten Shinto shrine.

Halo sat on the mossy paving stones. He could feel the heat and humidity lurking behind the walls and behind the thick leaves, but it was unable to penetrate this cool retreat. He was grateful and drank the strong, bitter coffee. The murky pool that was his mind was clearing as the ripples of caffeine brushed over the waters. His last memory was of the party he had attended many nights ago. It had been a wild, excessive gathering that had deteriorated into a bizarre game of Russian roulette. The polished silver gun had been passed around, and the hollow click of each chamber had echoed ominously as the gun was handed from one to another. Four clicks and the gun sat in Halo's hand. He caressed the metal grooves intimately, snorted another line of cocaine, and placed the nozzle against his temple. It nestled amid his curls like a jewel, and the room became very hushed. He pulled the trigger. The click of the hollow chamber reverberated amid the assembled.

He threw the gun down and it skidded across the glass coffee table, demolishing the neat parallel lines of powder. A gorgeous redhead picked it up, its gleaming surface now coated with narcotic dust. She delicately began licking it. The party had exploded into a kaleidoscope of throbbing lights and ear busting music. How many days had it been? Halo tried to figure it out, but time remained elusive. One thing he was sure of was that the figure that was still lying in his bed was a certain redhead with a cascade of curls reaching down her back. She had stayed the distance. What was her name? Azûrâ – that was her name – Azûrâ with a z.

He finished the coffee and stared at the black stalks of the bamboo. He wanted some space, so he slipped into the bedroom, grabbed a tee shirt and a pair of jeans, hastily dressed and headed for the door that took him to the basement garage and his dad's prized ecopod.

He drove down the sun blasted streets –the traffic was awful. The sky above was smeared with poisonous orange flares against the murky blue, and the smell of smoke came through the air-conditioning filter. Halo took one of the tunnels, following the flashing red signs, and pulled up beside one of the more respectable underground drive-throughs. It sold organic food, but somehow it still tasted plastic. Halo finished it and drove off, not really caring where it took him and ended up back outside – this time he wasn't sure where he was. He must've taken a wrong turn. Halo cruised now-empty streets and wasn't really surprised when he turned the corner and saw the twenty-foot high barbed-wire fence and the checkpoint. He eased the ecopod into where they directed.

"Sorry officer, I think I might be lost," Halo murmured as he showed his ID.

He followed their directions, driving down a road that wasn't quite deserted, for a slim dark-haired figure was walking carefully among the potholes. For a moment she reminded Halo of Jinja. The girl was almost at the corner when a ray of light spot lit her form and she vanished from his sight. The ecopod cruised to the corner, but what lay on the other side was just another deserted street, virtually identical.

He sped up; kicking up the dust and swiftly drove away. He was surprised that within a few blocks he was in familiar territory. He had not realised the Ghostlands were so close. Memories of Jinja and her brother Takiyo fell into his thoughts – vivid and real, it had only been a year since he had been living in Tokyo. Jinja was obsessed with books, actual books made of paper and cardboard, and held together with glue and thread, with fingerprints smearing the pages, and creases running like wrinkles along the side, she had a small collection; her special ones. She was obsessed with one particular book, 'The Magus,' and she talked about visiting the Greek islands, even though she knew most of them were now underwater. Still, she dreamed of Phraxos, and Lemonos, Naxos, Kos, Skyros. She whispered their names when he held her in his arms and kissed her. Tinos, Thassos, Zakynthos, and Icaria, she said as she ran her long, finely boned fingers through his thick, wavy hair.

***

He was home far quicker than he'd anticipated. Halo opened the door and found the place fresh and airy. All the blinds were up, the windows were open, and a cool breeze pervaded the rooms. Everything looked clean and tidy. A bunch of jessamine sat in a vase on the dining room table, and he could hear the faint hum of the dishwasher and washing machine coming from the other room. His first horrified thought was that his parents had come home early. They were not due home for another few months or had time sped by so quickly? He walked into the kitchen and noted everything was also cleaned and tidy. A bowl of fresh fruit sat on the bench. He opened the fridge. It was certainly stocked with more than it had been. There was a carton of milk, some cheese, a round loaf of fresh bread, and a couple of cans of beer. He turned when he heard footsteps. Azûrâ stood in the doorway. She was wearing a pair of his sister's faded jeans and a white tee shirt. Her red curls were tied back in a ponytail, her face was totally free of any make-up, and she looked very wholesome and pretty.

"You owe me," she said. "I'm sure I'll get it off you somehow. Dinner might be a good way, tonight." She smiled at him confidently from halfway across the room. "Grab a beer." Her voice trailed over to him; "join me, I'm sitting in the courtyard."

Halo wandered into the bedroom; the bed had been made and the sheets had been changed. His clothes that had been strewn all over the floor were bundled into an almost-tidy pile.

I suppose I'd better wash them soon, he thought.

The bathroom almost sparkled and the whirring of the washing machine lent a homely, domesticated feel to the place. Halo splashed his face with water and washed his hands with a newly opened bar of soap. He ran his hands over his unshaven face and decided to leave it until later. There probably wasn't any shaving cream, anyway, and then he noticed the bar of shaving cream. Was there anything she had forgotten to buy? What sort of girl was she? He thought she was some sort of party animal and here she was acting like a proud house frau.

Halo grabbed a beer, opened it and took a long drink, finding the coolness and the malt flavours curative, and wandered out to the courtyard. Azûrâ was slouched comfortably in a director's chair she had pulled out. Her head was thrown back, and her eyes were shut. She looked good sitting there among the dark greens of the vegetation – as though she belonged. Halo found the thought disturbing.

"You've made yourself very much at home," he said rather too sharply.

"Correction," Azûrâ replied, her eyes still shut, "I've made it into a home again. It was turning into a pigsty."

"That's not your problem, is it?"

"It is, if I'm going to be spending time here." Azûrâ opened her eyes and looked straight at Halo. Her eyes were very brown, an edible chocolate kind of brown; a delicious brown.

"What makes you think you will be spending time here?" he asked, but his tone had shifted, it was much lighter.

She smiled.

Halo looked at her pale white hands. "You didn't do any of this, did you?"

Azûrâ laughed, "of course not. I called in the hired help. They weren't doing anything, anyway."

She lifted the can and took a long, deep drink. Her throat was very white and at its base was a splattering of dusky freckles. Halo was beginning to remember those freckles – and the rest of her body very well. The long white limbs, the small patches of delightfully speckled skin like the eggshell of some exotic bird. He remembered the hot curls that threatened to suffocate him, her soft lips, and her little pink tongue that had slid around his body. He moved his gaze onto the mossy rocks and the moist, wet fronds of the unfurling ferns.

"I feel like Japanese tonight," her voice chimed into the stillness. For some reason, he felt a cold shiver run down his spine.

Chapter Four

Heart! We will forget him! You and I – tonight
You may forget the warmth he gave – I will forget the light!

Emily Dickinson

Raven sat up in bed – bolt upright – as though a sound or a movement had awoken her. This section of the rambling mansion was quiet. Raven sat in the darkness feeling her way through the emotions that were coursing through her being. If a noise had not disturbed her, then what had? For something had surged through her subconscious, something had caused her to wake like this with her heart pounding, and her breath shallow. She shook the bedclothes off and stood up; parting the curtains, she looked down to the street below.

Then it started again. It was like a wave that slowly rose from the ocean's depths, gaining momentum and power as it skimmed over the surface of Raven's being. It rose higher and higher, pulling her into it until she was nothing but a molecule of water, a single drop in its mighty flood. Then it crashed over her; the roar of its voice filled her mind, and the turbulence lifted her soul and spun her around. It suspended her in space and dropped her through a thousand starless nights. It threw her up into the billowing, foaming shallows and she emerged dripping, dishevelled, and on her knees. Around her, the waters swirled in a whirlpool, and she felt the pulling of the next wave as it demanded her presence.

It was a summoning.

Raven reached for the windowsill and used it as a lever to haul herself up from where she had fallen. She felt her heart beating against her chest, and the pull of the current as though it would rip her heart out of her body if she did not follow. This was what had aroused her from her slumber. In a daze, she dressed, pulling on her jeans and jumper. She unlocked her door and quickly descended the staircases that led to the huge foyer, which was unusually quiet even at this predawn time. She unlocked the massive wooden door and glided through like a sleepwalker. Along the overgrown path, where the disorderly bushes rustled and whispered and seemed to reach out talon-like branches snagging her hair, she approached the wrought-iron gate, already open as though the calling had affected it as well and, being an obedient servant, had prepared the way. Wraithlike, she floated down the early morning streets, which seemed unnatural in their total lack of movement. She was alone except for the invisible current that bound her and drew her as tightly and as forcefully as any rope. But who pulled the rope? Who demanded her presence?

Raven knew the answer. She had blocked it from her mind, refusing to believe or acknowledge its existence – as though if she erased it from her thoughts, it would soon flutter to the floor like a dead leaf and be blown away. Denial – it had always worked for her in the past – surely it would this time? Five long days had passed since her strange night in the warehouse. Five long days where she had constructed those walls she was so good at building – walls that would protect her and conceal her. She numbed her senses, blanked her memory, and played mental chess games over and over again, always avoiding the knight on his steed – until the board was overrun with white and black chess horses that ran in a wild zebra pack, and she had to slam that door shut too.

Five long days it waited for her to succumb willingly. And on the sixth day it lost patience.

Through the Ghostlands, she wafted like a spirit, until she found herself among the long grass and debris of the front yard of her warehouse. Heavy storm clouds obscured the waning moon, it was the dark side of morning, and dawn was many hours away. A movement of light caught her eye and she saw the beast emerge from the shadows. The mane was long and white, the body a grainy, sandy white that seemed to glow like the phosphorous on a wild beach. There was a shadow on the forehead as though a sharp-pointed knife had pierced the whiteness. The eyes were shadowed, but she could feel their gaze upon her.

There was an aura of power about this creature, but it was new and untested, and it used it carelessly and indiscriminately. Raven moved closer and the beast reacted by pawing the ground, it's hard hooves mashing the grass. The eyes glared at her and the voice, echoing through her mind, was a wind of wild fury. She looked into those eyes –they were darker than the night. Then the fury abated, and all was quiet.

This moonlit visage moved silently towards her, and she felt the soft nose nuzzle her hand. She stroked the velvety face and felt the sharp-edged point that protruded from the forehead. She couldn't see it, only as a shadow that darkened the white brow – it seemed invisible or perhaps because it was the same colour as the night, just obscured. She could feel it, like glass – very smooth, very hard, and very cold. It disturbed her so she moved her hand to the lovely silky mane that floated around her fingers like some diaphanous translucent material. She heard the voice in her mind, and out of the whispered language she couldn't understand, she picked a chord of music that reformed in her mind into syllables and resonances that were more familiar.

"Ceriful," she murmured. It had a strange sound, but it reminded her of stars falling, comets swirling, and ice breaking. It captured the unfathomable depths and brought them to the surface. A circle that endlessly continued – no beginning, no end.

The beast came closer, and the two leaned against each other. She, so dark and slight, a mere shadow; and he (for he was male, most definitely) so pale and misty – a moon beast. These two stood together, silently communicating in a language that belonged to neither, but was an amalgam of both. She heard his words of silver, and he heard her words of copper, and together they swirled around, transforming into something new – like a strange brew in an alchemist's chalice.

Chapter Five

And the Souls of whom thou lovest
Walk upon the winds with lightness,
Till they fail, as I am failing.
Dizzy, lost, yet unbewailling!

Percy Bysshe Shelley

"What are you doing out so late, little girl?"

"Just been out."

"Don't you know the dark can be dangerous? Full of vampires, werewolves and worse."

"I always carry a knife."

The streetlight shone dimly on the girl's face, putting half of it in shadow as though she wore a strange mask

"So, you think you are protected? Then why don't you hop in?"

Halo offered her a Hemplite cigarette. Raven took it and he lit it using Azûrâ's lighter, which was as thin as a surgical scalpel.

"Where are you going?"

The glow of the flame lit up Raven's eyes.

"To a bar, to hear someone sing. You want to come?"

He clicked the lighter shut. Raven's face was once again divided by the shadows.

Without a word, she walked around to the passenger side and got in. As the door slammed shut, Halo hit the accelerator and they took off. Raven could feel Ceriful tugging at the back of her mind, and behind him the clamouring of the endless buzzing of the world.

Halo's name had been at the door, and he convinced the security that there must've been some oversight that his guest hadn't been added. He mentioned Azûrâ and they let them both through. The lift, a red gleaming contraption with a ceiling of stars, moved so fast, Raven felt light-headed.

"This is pretty fancy."

He smiled and said; "you look great Raven. That corset is very retro-steampunk."

She laughed.

"At least we look like we're from the same tribe," he added.

"Is that important?" she asked.

"It might be."

Raven felt a strange falling sensation, as though the floor had suddenly given way, and a huge bottomless pit had opened under her feet. The lift stopped and they walked into an enormous room of glass, including the roof. She felt as if they were suspended in the night sky.

They brushed past bodies clothed in acres of midnight lace and blood velvet, the faces were paler than starlight, and as cruel and immobile as a stillborn child. The thought struck Raven that they were all so very young, yet already so close to death, that she could sense the shadow of the scythe falling lightly on their cheeks, dusting it with dark rouge. She felt suffocated by them – by their opulent garb and their indifferent thoughts. She wanted to run past them, shouting and screaming something, anything that would awaken them, but she couldn't think of the words. Apathy and torpor hung like thick cobwebs in the air – a trap, or a refuge – or both.

Halo ordered at the bar, shots of black liquor that made her gasp and her eyes dilate. She realised her head was silent. She pulled her phone out. The screen was dark. She looked around; the place must be shielded; only that could explain the silence in her head. No wonder the atmosphere was so strange. No diversions, these people were here with each other and no one else. No escape. No connecting to the outside or what they all thought was outside, but which was just another version of how they wanted their reality to be.

They are all probably going mad, she thought.

Suddenly, music filled the space; a large horn section and two pianos. The syncopation was ska-jazz with Goth reggae undertones. The singer – a tall girl with flaming red hair piled above her head – was dressed in a black and silver slim-line suit. Her voice ranged from kittenish sulky to a high-pitched roar. The place erupted with light; sheets of scarlet fell from the opaque ceiling like a blood waterfall. The Zombie Clique began dancing, lurching and swaying, spinning faster, weaving between each other, their lacy clothes fluttered around them, tinged with shadows of ichor.

"Is she your girlfriend?" Raven asked as they watched the singer.

Halo smiled; "I wouldn't go so far as that."

Her last song was done without words. She picked up a saxophone that had been hidden behind the amplifier. She played superbly. The rest of the band stopped – only the sax continued playing, filling the room with its sound, until it seemed like this glass cage might crack with the melancholy sadness of the music. The last note hung momentarily in the air. She held the saxophone in one hand and bowed. As she exited, the audience reacted with cheering and clapping.

A few minutes later, one of the black-garbed attendants escorted them to the VIP section; it was ringed with golden chains, and on one table a fountain of ebony liquid bubbled and smoked.

Azûrâ took Halo's hand and leaned in and kissed him.

She looked at Raven and said; "aren't you going to introduce us?" Her lips were silver.

Halo made the introductions and Azûrâ whisked him further into her entourage. Raven took a seat on a Mad Hatter chair; striped purple and white. The endless glass was behind her. She turned and stared beyond the reflections into the darkness. Amid the glittering skyscrapers and the shifting holographic advertising, the night sky was alive with eerie sights. Ephemeral spirits flew across the spaces between the buildings like strange-winged birds. Raven blinked and wondered if she was the only one seeing this. She looked back into the crowd. A man in a polymorphic mask, that oscillated into abstract colours as he breathed, was staring at her. His body was draped in silk, so sheer and tight; he may as well be naked. She felt a hot breath beside her ear and heard Ceriful speak to her in his secret language that she was only beginning to understand. She felt herself go dizzy, and the room began to spin in a kaleidoscope of colour and smoke. His whispers ebbed back to a pool of gentle ripples.

Raven got up and went to the bathroom. The room was gunmetal chrome and black steel with mirrors that shifted between clear and opaque. She looked at a face that was fragmented and somehow unfamiliar.

"I feel like that," Raven muttered to herself. "Inside, I feel just like that."

***

"She's a Carnie isn't she?"

"So?"

"Well, you know what they say; swipe your code faster than you can input your drawdown," Azûrâ replied, lifting one eyebrow as she stared at Halo. "Is that what you two do? Hack off together?"

"Shouldn't believe everything that is out there." Halo replied.

"Your dirty little secret is safe with me," Azûrâ whispered. "I won't tell."

Raven walked back into the area, an attendant moved the golden chains to let her in, and they clinked in a jarring wrong-pitched tone.

Azûrâ beckoned her over and patted the seat beside her. "Do you need something to drink or eat? There are loads of edibles around."

Raven shook her head. "I enjoyed your set."

"It's such a good feeling to be up there," Azûrâ looked at Raven, and shifted closer. Raven felt she was a specimen caught in the gaze of a curious, possibly malevolent scientist. "There's this feeling of power and exhilaration. You have the power, and they have the excitement, or maybe it's the other way round. But what happens is you transfer it between you, back and forth until this energy becomes something else, something even stronger. It's a symbiotic relationship. You feed on each other, and if you, the singer, are strong then you get to feed more and gain that energy. But if the audience are more powerful – or perhaps just disinterested – then they feed on you, and you give and give until you become a shell. It's very vampiric."

"So, you fed well?"

"Oh, very well. I feasted. Although the crowd is small, they make up for it in enthusiasm," Azûrâ licked her teeth dramatically. "I need to go and feast again."

She kissed Halo – a long, passionate kiss that left a smear of silver on his mouth.

They watched her walk to the stage.

Halo smiled at Raven and asked; "drink?"

She nodded and he stood up, walked to the bubbling fountain and dipped two silver cups in and brought them back. Raven was staring beyond the glass; there was a thin, stick-like, misty wraith slithering along, eyes' black and bottomless. She had seen it before, but this time she felt safer. It was out there, and she was in here. Its gossamer garments streamed behind it like some flimsy cloak. It looked at her and opened its mouth; its teeth were extremely sharp and pointed. She looked away. Halo passed her a cup, drops of the jet liquid slithered down the outside. It looked poisonous, nevertheless she sipped it, surprisingly it was quite tasty, a sweet herbaceous flavour.

Halo was looking at Raven, feeling something was different, it was an impression, it was invisible, but he could perceive it nevertheless. It was like the wind, only seen in the way it affected things around it; leaves quivering, boughs bending, flags fluttering. Something was affecting Raven, some current flowed around her. Halo had felt it brush against him tentatively, a cool almost-fluid like feeling, his skin reacting momentarily to something alien, unknown.

He leaned over and asked; "are you ok?"

She gave him a strange look; "I'm fine."

"Do you want to go outside for a while?"

She shook her head. She looked over to where Azûrâ was singing a duet with one of the guitarists. The guitarist had an almost angelic face, especially when he sang. She looked at the crowd; they were swaying together, almost as if they were one organism. She suddenly felt very lonely.

"Have you been back?" he asked.

She turned and looked at him, trying to discern his meaning. Then she understood.

"Yes," she replied, finally.

"Have you seen anyone else there?"

She thought about the riders in the slipstream; she didn't know what they were, wasn't even sure now what she had seen. Maybe it was her imagination? "I don't think so. But how would I know. It was just chance that we were there together."

She still didn't know how they had recognised each other that time. It's not like they were anything that substantial; or even identifiable, certainly not human, except perhaps an echo or a heartbeat – the remnant of a shadow. Yet they had known – they had recognised each other. Somehow, among the glowing colours and shapes, they had some recognisable imprint. Then they had been compelled, yes that was the word, she thought, they had been compelled to meet afterwards and, somehow acknowledge what had happened, where they had been – even though it was almost impossible to describe it.

"How do you do it?" he asked.

"You mean how do I find the way in?"

He nodded, although what he really meant to ask was how do you do it, and not lose some intrinsic part of yourself? How do you do it and not fall into that swirling star stream, surrendering to it, letting everything, including your sanity, go? But maybe that was an unfair call.

"It's there, isn't it? The in-between space, you just slip in," she replied.

It wasn't easy; she knew that. Most people stayed within very narrow confines of the web, places that were easily accessible. Those sites that were enjoyable, shopping, chatting, and entertainment – even if you travelled into the darker alleys, you would still not necessarily find it. Was it because they were both trawlers, slipping within and between the coding and the interfacing? That was her job. And Halo? For enjoyment, she presumed – and because he could – because, like her, it was something easy that came almost naturally to him.

Raven looked at him; the coloured lights were creating patterns on his face. He was watching her, the way he would, quietly with interest, as though the looking was another form of communication between them. And maybe it was.

"Do you ever wonder about slipping out? Well, about not slipping out? Because it's very seductive in there isn't it? How easy would it be to just stay?" he murmured.

"Could you stay?" she asked. "The connection would break at some point. You'd lose power, your device would turn off and that would be it."

Even as she said it, she realised that wasn't true. The last time she hadn't been connected, there was no signal on her phone. She had gone in without using any device. She had just entered the slipstream somehow, by herself. She swallowed and felt a wave of coldness close over her. How was that possible?

Chapter Six

There was the Door to which I found no Key:
there was the veil which I might not see.

Omar Khayyam

The Past

Jo wandered around her apartment; it was a basement flat, small, airless, claustrophobic. She shared the space with Zento, a reclusive poet who webweaved for nameless corporations. Their relationship was based on a mutual dislike for superficial chitchat; they could go for weeks without uttering a word, then spend a night pouring out their disturbances like a dam bursting over.

Jo stalked the rooms, frustrated, annoyed. She heard the bars of the front entrance open and then the slide of the card. There was a jarring sound. She turned, expecting to see Zento but instead saw two strangers. Jo fell to the floor with the scent of roses in her nostrils and the thought that there really wasn't anything worth stealing.

She awoke to the stinking smell of refuse, her body was damp and felt broken and battered, the white corona of a copter light was pounding her optic nerves, and she heard the thumping of its blades. She felt arms covered in anti-contaminate gloves lift her onto something that felt very soft. She looked into a set of dark, sad eyes and heard a familiar voice swearing.

I really should do something about these rescue fantasies, she thought before she lost consciousness again.

They sat together on the rooftop watching the bleary sky turn red and orange, and a bizarre shade of purple; a bruise is what it reminded her of.

I sit looking at a sunset and all I see are bruises, Jo thought. Connor smoked his cigarette and stared morosely at the horizon of skyscrapers. *The gargoyle and I, on the edge,* she mused, *all we need is to be turned to stone, two gargoyles together, forever.*

"What are you thinking?" he asked.

"The total transience of everything," she replied flippantly.

"Some things can't be destroyed."

"Like what?"

"Evil."

"Don't be going religious on me now."

"Religion has no monopoly on evil. Evil is. It's just out there, like the air, like the toxins. You can't see it, but you feel the consequences."

Jo made no reply as she stared at the sky; the bruised skin of the stratosphere, sick with accumulated poisons.

The planet's dying, she thought sadly.

"There are too many strange threads. I'm being led around the labyrinth and it's not by your average sociopath weirdo – no this is something more orchestrated and subtle," Connor began, as he turned and looked at Jo. "Get too close and the hall of mirrors bounces up and you can't tell which reflection is real, and which isn't. Decoys. Traps. Deceptions." Connor paused.

He blinked and his voice dropped lower with a hint of bitterness; "there's also what happened to you. You were asking too many questions. We found a derivative of BDA in you. You know what that means? They wanted to know how much you knew. It's a good thing you're pretty much immune to all of that."

Jo's face was set in hard lines. Her eyes were the palest of blue like cats-eye marbles. She had a face that reminded Connor of raw quartz. It was all impossible angles and edges; it was crystalline white – and somehow reflective, like ice. If he ran his hand over her skin, would it be smooth and warm, or hard and cold? He had a vision of her naked on a lake of ice; the white blonde of her hair and skin blending into the frozen glacial landscape. He blinked that visual shut.

The sky was almost dark, and Connor's face was in shadow. "Ever heard of Tierra Del Fuego?"

"South America?"

"It translates to Land of Fire. It's something that keeps cropping up," Connor paused, looking thoughtful. "When I was a child, my father used to drive me out to a petrochemical plant. To look at the dragon, he'd say. The dragon was this tall chimney made of blackened steel that had a perpetual, burning flame. It made the weirdest sound, like a breathing beast, a wheezing, rasping noise. My father called this place the Land of Fire."

"Does it still exist?" she asked.

"Feel like a drive?" he stood up.

***

Connor parked his pod. The petrochemical plant was deserted, the dragon long dead. Only its skeleton reared starkly into the sky. The enormous tanks were empty and some had crumpled into themselves. Jo had fallen asleep on the drive over, he gazed at her, entranced.

Why do I always think of fairy stories when I look at her? He wondered, those long forgotten fairy stories from his childhood. The Snow Queen, Sleeping Beauty; she had been Rapunzel the first time he saw her, when her hair was so long. Yet he knew her to be formidable – mentally and physically. She looked so desirable as she slept, and he wanted, almost desperately, to lean over and kiss her.

Not a good idea, he thought, *not now, probably not ever.*

He had no misconceptions about his looks. Reality comes early to ugly ducklings and not all grow into beautiful swans.

He climbed out leaving her sleeping; Connor often felt he lived his life in the darkness. Perhaps it was for the best; the night suited his face, the dark was full of scary beasts, monsters, and creatures ugly and misshapen. He walked on feet used to treading softly, panther steps; predatory almost. He heard the sounds first, low drone of human voices, machinery. He found them too easily.

They are too confident, he thought, until he felt the cold steel against his head.

The sentry led him through the jagged doorway cut into the now-empty tank. The inside was cavernous, concave, and hollow. There was no sign of a roof, just an immense yawning blackness, and a smell of old gasoline. Lamps on the floor lit the way to where the ten people sat on chairs around a long steel table; Connor heard the sound of a baby crying, far away. He noticed how well dressed they were; corporate, conservative capitalists around a board table.

"Congratulations." An immensely tall man stood up from the table, his voice boomed in the empty chamber. He smiled, a serpentine smile. He looked like a Viking in a suit.

"You don't know who we are, do you?"

"Well, I guess you aren't Rapturists."

The Viking laughed. "No, we are definitely not them. We're scientists, geneticists, and climatologists. You are privileged to see the inner core – a rare event. I hope you appreciate the situation."

"I'm overwhelmed."

"You should be. We are the future of this fucked up planet."

"Why does that fill me with unease?"

The Viking laughed, yet his eyes were chillingly cold.

"What's the baby got to do with it?" Connor asked bluntly.

"Straight to the point, I like that. The baby's only importance is its genetic make-up," The Viking beamed, his teeth were too perfect. "Purely because of her father, he was one of our own, he began us. We follow his charter. He unfortunately died in an accident off the coast of South America, his body swept away in a catastrophic storm."

"Tierra Del Fuego," Connor whispered. He heard a rasping, slippery sound. "Why kill the mother?"

"Expediency, of course. We have limited time, and people can be so difficult. Wouldn't you agree? And now we have another problem, don't we?"

"Don't mind if I smoke, do you?" Connor reached into his suit pocket, felt the man's hand on his arm before he even saw him move.

"I don't think so, not good for the health, and we all are on a tight deadline here, we have flights waiting. You will have to excuse us." He motioned to the burly sentry. "Stefan, escort the detective off the premises. Somewhere discreet should do."

Connor heard the rasping sound again, slightly closer.

"What happens to the baby?"

"She will be taken care of. We are not barbarians. And it is not your problem." The Viking's voice had an impatient edge to it.

Connor stared at the man. "Really? I've seen barbarians with more respect for life than you've shown."

"Don't try and bait me, Inspector, I've faced far bigger players than you'll ever know."

Connor let Stefan escort him out; he felt a rush of a wind and he instinctively hit the floor, but not before he saw her abseil down from the darkness like some vengeful angel. Her boots hit Stefan's head as she somersaulted onto the ground. Stefan fell with a thud. Connor picked up the pistol that had skittered across to him, and they dragged the body into the shadows. He pulled out his phone. There was no signal.

"I think I know where they are. This way," Jo said as she switched her tiny pinprick torch on and led him into a gaggle of pipes, twisting gleaming copper, the entrails of a dragon.

The pipes contorted and coiled into a vast network; in one of the circular chambers, they found the baby asleep with her two guardians. A dimmed lantern swung above them, the woman's body covered by a snake tattoo that coiled over her; intricate and more complete than the gauzy garment she wore. The young man was short and misshapen. His limbs looked deformed, as though they had been broken and repaired by a drunken surgeon. There was something peaceful about the way the three lay together. Jo bent over to pick up the baby.

"No!" a harsh voice echoed out of the darkness.

The two sleeping figures woke up abruptly; the woman stood up in a graceful, almost dancelike motion. She grabbed the baby, staring at Jo defiantly. Three men now stood behind Jo and Connor, one of them was holding a steel rod and beating it against the palm of his other hand.

"The deal is off. You tell that to your leader. He already owes us too much, and I'm not happy with the bullshit I'm hearing."

Connor replied slowly, winging it. "Money is not an issue, you know that."

"It's not the money. It's all the other broken promises. His manifesto changes depending on who he's talking with. We'll keep the baby, if he starts to give us what he promised, I'll be in contact."

All of them faded away into the blackness.

"Dissension in the ranks," Jo remarked.

"Seems like it." Connor said.

"What now?"

"Let's find a place we can get phone coverage."

The copters came long before they could call it in; they watched them, their lights flickering like a swarm of giant fireflies. They disappeared into the vast complex of pipes and vats, and a few minutes later they took off again, heading away from them.

"I doubt if we would've had enough to pin anything on them," Connor said, "especially with the baby gone."

***

Jo watched the dawn from the rooftop. The sky was grey, cloudy, and forlorn, it matched her mood. *I've been lonely for too long*, she thought.

She heard his footsteps and turned. His face was tired, haggard, his eyes world-weary. Connor lit a cigarette and passed over a flask of alcohol.

What the hell, she thought as she drank it. It was good quality; very smooth.

"Ongoing?" she asked and passed the flask over.

Connor shook his head; "in our own time though." He looked at her. "Officially, you are off the payroll."

"I always have spare time. As long as we share the information."

"The Viking's name is Mars Lodstrom. He is now the sole director of the Heimdallr Institute, as the other director Sebastian van Elson died onboard the ship off the coast of Tierra Del Fuego.' It's a scientific think tank, as you'd expect. They are the main advisory body to the World Earth Future Forum, and between the climatologists, geneticists, meteorologists and virologists, they are crucial and therefore very powerful. Mars is virtually untouchable. Even asking for a very low-key surveillance on him, they knocked me back as it being too invasive, and there is no actual evidence he is involved."

"Any leads where the baby might be?"

"Disappeared into the underworld, it seems. Those five we met in the entrails of the dragon are most likely Carnies. As a small but growing-larger-every-nano-second criminal gang, they run the entertainment quarters, nightclubs, bars, strip joints, brothels, real world and online. And, if the information I've heard is correct, they also run the biggest hacking syndicate there is." Connor paused for a moment. "That's where the mega money is. They are slowly annihilating their competition, not in the old-fashioned blood bath killing way, but by dismantling and infecting their competitor's online presence with viruses and malware. Apparently, their software is very cutting edge; it buries deep and mutates, almost impossible to clean up."

"I've come across them, very hard to infiltrate, it's all networked around tribal ties. If you aren't verified by at least twenty people, you cannot even get a shithole job with them, let alone access to anyone else," Jo replied. "What about that dead doctor in the crashed pod, found not far from the apartments; what Intel did you end up with?"

"Not a Carnie, that's for sure. Not much on him, no criminal activity, not even a parking fine. Came from a good family, he was trained in obstetrics, but his experience was minimal. There was blood on him that matched the victim. He was there, almost definitely not alone, there were others."

Connor paused and took a swig of his flask before he continued. "Although the crash killed him, he had some unexplainable lacerations. Some animal attacked him; maybe more than one; there were gouges and slashes all over him, especially his hands and face. Some sort of canine probably, but no DNA was found, which is weird. That amount of clawing and biting should leave salvia traces."

"What caused the crash?" Jo asked.

"Another mystery, something caused him to drive so erratically that he lost control and went over that embankment. And nothing in the pod to show the baby was ever in it, again implying that he wasn't working alone." Connor shook his head.

"The unofficial verdict is a botched caesarean, the baby missing. At least there was enough of the placenta to provide her DNA for future identification. I'm calling it murder still and following any lead that comes up but…." Connor said with some bitterness, as he took another swig from the flask.

She looked at him keenly.

"There's something you still haven't told me though. You going to fill me in?"

When he finally spoke, it was a hushed whisper, grey and foggy like the morning.

"The dead woman was my sister."

She stared at his face. It was tragic, gothic, drained of everything, drained of life. It had become like stone; a real gargoyle at last. Yet somehow, despite it all, it became beautiful, like an object ruined beyond hope can still maintain the essence of what it was.

"My mother deserted us when I was seven. She ran away to join the Rapturists. I never saw her again. A few years ago, I began to do some investigating and discovered I had a half sister. I found out what I could about her, but that was it. I only knew her from a file until the day I stepped into her apartment and saw her dead on the floor."

He's lonelier than I am, Jo thought.

Connor ground out his cigarette on the stone parapet; the gesture was dismal and final. He stared at the scrapers rising from the fog. His hands were stuffed into the pockets of his jacket. He looked ready to leave.

I really want him, she thought, *and if I don't make a move now it will never happen. It's only my pride, and maybe fear that's stopping me.*

She leaned over and kissed him. She felt his surprise and then he had his arms around her, caressing her hair, murmuring softly, kissing her back fiercely and with a passion unlike anything she had experienced before.

Chapter Seven

The Present

Twilight was casting its mauve-grey light on the world, the shadows were deepening, and the cool breeze blowing up from the bay was alleviating the heat. Here, in the Ghostlands, all was very calm and still; the deserted buildings sat like rusty relics among the dry grass and dust. Grasshoppers skipped between the weeds and the broken bottles, and lizards awoke from their slumbers, lying on the warmed rocks and rusty machinery, their eyes searching for predators.

Raven sat on her familiar couch of canvas that had moulded with her form. Her beast lay next to her; his white head and neck rested in her lap, his whiteness a striking contrast to her black outfit, his mane that flowed to the floor was a shimmering radiant waterfall, and his ebony horn was sharp and dangerously long, and very cold to the touch. Ceriful's eyes were closed as though he was sleeping, and his very long golden lashes fluttered gently. Raven stroked his soft fur that had an almost skin-like texture, and she entangled her fingers in his mane that felt like threads of silk. She wondered how could he be real, he felt solid and alive. And, if he was real, did that mean the other forms she saw were real too? She didn't want to think about that.

"Where do you come from?" she whispered.

"From behind the veil."

She heard his voice in her mind; it flowed like water and was cool like a shadowy forest. She was used to his presence and now only occasionally would she feel dizzy when she felt the echoing of his words.

"I don't understand."

"Behind the veil, the veil that hides all the worlds that exist from each other. The gossamer that separates your world from mine."

"Where is it?"

"It is everywhere. It is nowhere."

"That doesn't make sense."

"Only if you believe it doesn't."

"Can you see it?"

"If you know how to look. If you know when to look."

"You mean where to look?"

"No, I mean when to look. Between the light and shadow, between one second and another you may catch a glimpse."

"How did you get here?"

There was silence.

"How will you get back?"

"When it is time, the veil will open, and I will slip through."

"How will you know?"

"I will know."

"Why are you here?"

"To find what I need that will complete my world. To find it and return with it."

"What are you looking for?"

"When I find it, I will know."

Ceriful opened his eyes and looked at Raven, but she was looking absently at the floor, or perhaps something beyond. His eyes were an amazing colour, like amethyst crystals cut in a way that made them seem to be almost on fire, or almost frozen, depending on the light. He observed Raven in a sly way, his lashes lowered slightly, as Raven looked up and met his glance.

"I do not die, I sleep and dream and reform when the conditions are right."

"So, you are very old? You have never died?"

"I have never died in the way that I see death in your mind, as for age it is a concept I do not understand. Your kind have invented so many ways of measuring and dissecting time. Time for me is meaningless, it just is. It exists and ebbs and flows continuously. Why do you need to bind it as you do?"

"I didn't realise we did."

Raven sat for a while, silently stroking Ceriful's mane. The warehouse was very shadowy now, the light had faded and the sky through the skylight was dark, only a lonesome star glimmered. Ceriful glowed in his whiteness illuminating Raven's face and the surrounding air.

Raven asked the question which had been on her mind for a long while.

"Can others see you?"

Ceriful laughed in her mind, his voice low and silky soft.

"Only if I allow them. Only if they choose."

"So, if they wanted to see you but you didn't want them to, they would not be able to."

"Seeing is always based on the unspoken permission of both parties."

"All seeing?"

"Of course. You would be surprised at how little others really see."

She thought about all the strange entities she saw. She wanted to ask about them but didn't, instead she asked if he needed to eat food.

"I live on the energy that others discard. Your kind is very wasteful. You discard constantly, your dreams, your visions, and your thoughts. In other worlds these things are treasured and cared for, but your kind seem to have found no use for them. I live off that vitality, it floats around and collects in the forgotten places. This place is full of discarded dreams, unremembered illusions, exquisite visions that are no longer wanted. Aspirations that have been shattered and thrown away, it's all here, and there is so much."

"You have been here before?"

"Yes. It was a while ago, in your measurements of time, perhaps, a few hundred years. I grew much more slowly. Dreams were more important then."

"Why do you come?"

"I told you; to find what I need."

"You always find it then?"

"Always."

"What would happen if you couldn't find it?"

"It is inconceivable."

"And this object that you will find, you will take it back with you."

"I did not say it was an object."

"What is it then?"

"An essence is a better way of defining it."

"Okay, this essence then, you will take it back with you but how will it save your world? Is it magic or something?"

Ceriful was thoughtful before he spoke. "It acts like osmosis; I become of this world as well as being alien to this world. The essence is like that – when I return with it, it coalesces with our world, and our world becomes different, charged with it. Each essence is quite unique and, as it flows through us, we are all subtly changed. It infuses us with something fresh, something new. Perhaps, that is the real magic of the essence."

"And this is how it always happens, you find, and you return, and all is renewed?"

"Yes."

"Does it ever not differ?"

"Only in the detail."

"What was it like, the last time? Do you remember?"

"I awoke in a place that was high on a mountain, a city that was built of hewn stone and all around the jungle was very close and very ravenous. It was a very hot place and every afternoon it would rain for hours, drenching the earth and the vines, then the heat would be almost suffocating like the air had turned to water; each gasp was like drowning. In the beginning, I lived in a cave but the energy that I needed to grow was very sparse, although the vegetation was so incredibly lush and succulent, it was quite ironic that I was forced to leave this abundant growth to find my nourishment elsewhere. I travelled through the jungle and in a small village; I met a maiden who became my guide. She carried me, as I was still so very small. She carried me until we came to the city where I found the energy, and I began to grow. These people held on to their dreams; visions and dreams were sacred to them, and they gave them up unwillingly. That was why it was so hard for me to sustain myself. Their visions were very dark, full of blood and sacrifice, portents of doom – for their destruction was near. They had seen it in the stars, their calendars were full of eschatological omens, and they sensed it all around them. Some even perceived me, although I had not allowed them to, so strong was their awareness of the growing climax that was to engulf them.

"My maiden was revered as someone holy, as she had been chosen by myself. There was an aura of purity about her. She had hair that fell to her ankles; it was a blackness that almost shimmered with blue, her skin was very dark like wild honey, and her eyes were, I can still remember them. Oh, they were a translucent, shimmering brown like smooth pebbles that lie on a creek bed, and as the water flows over them the sunrays are refracted by the liquid, and they seem to change colour, and almost become light. She was exceptional. But her city and her people were doomed. I could hear the army that was heading towards their dominions, I could feel their visions; so strong and fearless that it preceded their bodies like clouds announcing a mighty storm and, they believed their god was with them, they were conquering for him, as well as for the gold that they believed they would find. And there was much gold to find. But their dreams were as dark, perhaps even darker than these people that they so abhorred, and brutal, almost inhumanly cruel. I am glad that I did not need to stay and watch the final slaughter. The veil lifted before they entered the gates."

"The girl, what happened to her?"

"She was safe, I would not leave her for them to defile."

"So, am I your guide?"

"Do I really need to answer that?"

"But I don't take you anywhere, I don't show you anything."

"My maiden of the jungle was pure by the nature of her living for all her years within the confines of her natural environment. The huge-leaved vines and the warm rain, and the clear air had distilled a simplistic openness in her, she was almost an animal, almost a flower; she was totally natural and in tune with the world around her. She was as pristine as a mountain stream and as guiltless as the jaguar that kills to live. You are like that; but your world is quite different, your world is multi-dimensional, it exists within as much as without, what is real and what is not – there is little to differentiate it. Plastic, metal, machines, the airwaves and transmissions that circle your world like another atmosphere, and you have somehow incorporated them into the organic. You have joined with them."

Ceriful gazed at Raven and his violet eyes seem to burn through the darkness like a lilac flame.

And you my sweet, have merged with them in a way that is unlike any other, he thought to himself, swathing that thought so she couldn't hear.

Chapter Eight

*No moon in the still heaven, in the black water none,
the sins on her soul are seven, the sin upon his is one.*

Oscar Wilde

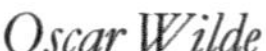

Halo parked the ecopod and although it was still early, he felt very tired and had just dropped Azûrâ off – they had been bickering, as they seemed to do increasingly regularly. Azûrâ had plans and wanted him to be part of them, but he was reluctant. There was something too arrogant about the way she assumed that he now belonged to her, as though he were a possession she had bought. And she wanted some sort of commitment but wouldn't really tell him exactly why, and what for. He was beginning to find her repellent.

He walked around the corner and straight into someone that was standing on the sidewalk, staring up at the gigantic two-headed monster that stood in the shallow water. The young woman was so deeply involved in studying the colourful mosaics that she almost didn't register him. He was so surprised at who she was, that he almost tripped again.

"Raven," Halo regained his composure.

"Hi."

He thought she looked tired, he noted the small dark circles under her eyes, bruising her pale, translucent skin. He wondered how she was spending her nights, with whom was she spending her nights?

"Didn't figure you were the cultural type," he said almost too bluntly, and then instantly regretted it. *I'm tired and snarky this morning*, he thought, *I shouldn't be around people.*

"Well, you never can tell," she answered without a hint of sarcasm. "What are you doing here?"

"I'm picking up something. What about you?"

Raven looked slightly bewildered as though she couldn't remember why she was here. Halo waited, he almost expected her to say that she was just passing but she hesitantly spoke.

"There's something I'm looking for. I thought I might find it in there."

"Like what?"

"I will know when I see it," Raven felt dizzy. Hadn't someone said those exact words to her only a few days ago? She staggered and Halo automatically reached out and steadied her, he held her arm and searched her face.

"Are you okay?"

"Fine."

Halo looked at her closely. She was probably just tired. She looked like she hadn't slept much. He presumed she was still trawling; after all it was what she did, it was her job, she was required to do it by the Carnies, he understood that much about them. What he really wanted to ask her was if she'd been into the slipstream, the name they had decided on to call that place, but just the thought of it made his chest constrict.

Instead, he asked; "shall we go in?"

They wandered through the massive foyer and then into the great halls and large rooms. Raven avoided the photographs and the glass sculpture and the modern abstract installations. She had little interest though Halo stopped, he liked the chaotic, anarchistic displays of colour, and the different mediums that the artists used: pieces of rusted wire, a cardboard box, spliced cans of Pepsi remade into something else.

They climbed the stairs and entered a world of old oils on canvas: Nineteenth, eighteenth, seventeenth century and beyond. The paintings were huge; romantic scenes of ancient legends, towering landscapes of magnificent mountains bathed in unearthly light, intricate details of daily life and death, voluptuous nude women lying on brocade couches clothed in soft shadows. Here was Christ dying on Calvary while the angels wept with operatic gestures. Another depicted the lord of the manor astride his horse; the carcass of a great stag slung over his lap, his hounds slavering and baying between the hooves of his mount.

Raven looked around frustrated, searching everywhere. They were now in the fourteenth and fifteenth centuries. Small gilt-encrusted frames showed iconic Madonna and child portraits.

On one wall a huge tapestry hung, castle turrets with fluttering flags, ladies gaily waving coloured scarves, knights in shining armour riding warhorses covered in matching silver plates, and thick woods where magical creatures roamed. Raven studied the forest and their inhabitants, a strange monkey-faced lion peered from behind a shrub, a phoenix rose from the ashes of a forgotten fire, a green salamander slunk into an emerald pond, a serpent twined around a tree that was shaped like a curvy woman, a three headed dog snapped and snarled at dragon flies that flew around his head. She searched, but it wasn't there.

They had reached the end of the floor and took the lift back to the ground floor lobby. Halo suggested that Raven have a look in the shop as he had finally recalled the reason he had come. He wandered over to the administration area. When he returned, Raven was sitting on a seat – she had bought something. They both were clutching small brown paper packages.

"Let's grab a coffee, I know I need one," Halo said.

They sat in the courtyard of the small café, it was sunny – sheltered from the unusually sharp southerly wind, miniature orange trees grew in terracotta pots, and swallows darted in and out of the cracks in the high wall. The air was surprisingly clear for a change. The place was almost deserted; they drank coffee and shared a bowl of chips.

"What did you buy?"

Raven looked up at him in surprise; "just a card."

"Can I see?"

She looked like she wanted to refuse, but she pushed the package over. He pulled the card out. It was a reproduction of a tapestry, not the one that hung in this gallery, but another. The colours were predominantly red, green and gold. In the centre sat a rather dour-faced maiden, she was seated between two trees; one was an oak full to bursting with acorns, the other tree was a holly, judging by the leaves, and it was covered in red berries. She had long golden-brown hair and her gown was richly decorated with leaves and flowers. In one hand, she held a round mirror with a thick golden stand, the other hand was draped over the neck of a unicorn. The unicorn was cream-coloured, and his long white horn burst out of his head an impossibly long way.

His eyes were playful and his front hooves rested on the lady's lap. He looked like a cross between a pony and a goat.

Halo read the inscription aloud; "La Dame a La Licorne – The Lady and the Unicorn.

"Was there a particular reason that you chose that one?" Raven shrugged.

"Poor thing. He doesn't realise he is going to be killed."

"What?" Raven exclaimed.

"The unicorn. He doesn't realise he's been lured to his doom."

"What do you mean?" Raven looked more awake and interested than she had all morning.

"You must know the story?" Halo asked.

"No. Tell me."

"Well, the only way to kill a unicorn is to trap it and ambush it. They can run very fast, and they are shy, elusive creatures that hide in the densest part of the forest. And the only trap that would guarantee that a unicorn would come out of its hiding place was a maiden. So, the hunters would pick the loveliest, purest – she had to be a virgin – maiden, and they would bring her into the forest, and leave her sitting demurely in a clearing. Then, the hunters would hide behind a tree and wait. The maiden would sit patiently, playing with her trinkets and singing softly, that was another plus – if she had a sweet voice then that would lure the unsuspecting creature in even more. They would wait, all day sometimes, and if they were lucky, the unicorn would emerge from the safety of the forest. It would see the lovely, virginal maiden and hear her sweet, pure voice and her beauty would overcome it and the unicorn wouldn't be able to resist the temptation to approach; to sit beside her and rest its head on her lap. Then, as it rested in perfect bliss, the hunters would jump out and either kill it with their swords, or capture it and sling it up, and take it back to the castle to be kept as part of the lord's menagerie where it would slowly wither, and die."

"That's horrible," Raven looked truly upset.

"It's only a story," Halo said casually.

"So did they really exist?"

"In the twelfth and thirteenth centuries people believed that they were real. There were lots of sightings, kind of like all the sightings of angelic aliens that occur now. When I was studying Jung, he theorised that all these sightings were just symbols of world consciousness given form. In the twelfth century people saw unicorns, in the nineteenth century people saw fairies and goblins, last century it was UFOs and flying saucers. It's all states of mind," Halo laughed, before continuing. "I've always found it interesting that it was virgins that were so compelling to unicorns. Why virgins? What is it about the state of virgins that is so over-powering? And unicorns aren't the only mythical creatures that prefer virgins, vampires are also said to prefer the blood of an unsullied, uncorrupted maiden. Even God supposedly picked a virgin to bear his child."

Halo winked at Raven who was still looking too serious. The waitress came by, and Halo ordered some juice.

He picked up the card and examined it, "look here." He pointed to the mirror the maiden held in her hand. "See how there is no reflection, even though the mirror is pointing directly at the unicorn. Proves my point."

"What point was that?" Raven asked smiling for the first time that day.

The sun was shining on her face highlighting her grey-blue eyes, the colour of the sea on a stormy day, and her lips were enticingly pouted. The glossy blackness of her hair, with that bluish lustre like the wing of the bird she was named after. She looked very alluring. She repeated her question.

"Oh. The point I was going to make," Halo said, pulling himself away from her face and all those unspoken and unacknowledged feelings that he kept very much below the surface. "Well, it's that, just like vampires, unicorns have no reflection, and this begs the question. Would God have a reflection? And if he didn't, what would that mean? Would that mean that God was a vampire? Or, perhaps, a unicorn even?"

Raven burst out laughing, and Halo was glad to hear the sound.

"So, the moral of the story is that if you are a virgin, you best lose your virginity as quickly as possible, then you have nothing to fear from unicorns, vampires and most importantly, God," he looked keenly at Raven and lifted one eyebrow.

She looked defiantly back as she said; "I understand the danger from vampires, and I can imagine how fearful it would be to be face to face with God, but what threat could a unicorn bring?"

"Mm, a most interesting question, I don't know, perhaps, they would be so unearthly, so beautiful and enchanting that nothing would be able to compare. Perhaps, they would steal away the desire to live."

"The desire to live," Raven repeated vaguely.

Raven sipped the remnants of her coffee that had grown cold. The bitter taste made her stomach turn.

"What's in you parcel?" Raven asked. "I've shown you mine."

"I was picking it up for my mother. I don't actually know what it is. A piece of her artwork I suppose," Halo gently pulled out a small box all taped up.

"Is she an artist?"

"It's a family secret," Halo smiled.

"What other family secrets are there?"

"Heaps," he winked.

She looked away, whenever she was with him, she felt a creeping sense of elation, and a kind of excitement that seemed to seep through her body, making her feel more hypersensitive than she already was. She remembered the first time she saw him; she had glanced up from her game of Go and seen him across the crowded courtyard, he was staring at her, and there was a moment of recognition on her part, like they knew each other, or had met before – yet she knew that wasn't the case because this moment was their meeting.

***

She had brought her focus back to her game, knowing that he was making his way over, and finding a spot to sit and watch. She'd won easily, her opponent getting up, nodding at her, and leaving. She was clearing the board – carefully collecting the black and white stones into separate piles. Halo had stood there, and, in a quiet voice with that sardonic hint of amusement that she got to like, had asked if he could play. She had asked if he knew how to play and he had said, 'of course, otherwise I wouldn't suggest it. Being totally annihilated by a such a good player as you so obviously are, is not my idea of a fun afternoon.'

She had won, but it had been demanding. They had played three more games, which she had won, but only because she pulled out every tactic she knew. After that, they caught up regularly playing Go, which after the seventh game between them he finally won; sometimes they played chess or even card games. He knew one of the Carnies who sold drugs and was obviously trusted enough to have been given a secret code to enter the mansion and hang out here, because he came more and more often, just to see her.

They began to talk, really talk; he was interested in what she did, who she was, what she thought, and he shared with her his world, so different from hers. She told him that her parents were dead, and she had ended up here, she was not considered a Carnie, as that was a birthright, she was a dalita, one of the scattered; without the birthtree showing her ancestors, even marrying a Carnie would not change her status. It meant her situation was precarious, and although she sensed that Halo wouldn't mind turning their association into something more, that was not anything she could consider, as it could easily make her seem less than she was now. So, she made sure she stayed within the bounds of a respectable friendship, and Halo made sure that he did too.

Chapter Nine

I tried to speak your poems but I could not!
The weeping of the gods fell upon my ears.

Masaoka Shiki

The Past – Japan

"I don't usually take on these commissions," Namiyo said as he led his visitor down the stairs to the room that looked out onto the deck with the large circular, carved sculptures. "Have a seat. Can I get you anything?"

"No, thank you." Tadahisa said as he fidgeted with the large, long bag he carried and placed carefully over his lap.

The two men were distantly related through both of their mothers and had met over the years; usually at big family weddings or funerals. So, when Namiyo had taken his phone call earlier in the day, it seemed impolite to not at least look at what it was that Tadahisa wanted from him. And he could always name a price so prohibitive that it would be enough to dissuade this distant relative.

"It's a katana that belonged to my great-grandfather and I need to commission a new handle, it has been stored badly and the tsuka has deteriorated to such a bad extent, that I have had to remove it." Tadahisa said; he paused and stared moodily outside. Dark storm clouds were brewing in the distance and the wind had come up, so the wooden window frames rattled. "It's my fault you see, I was supposed to be taking care of it and I left it somewhere I shouldn't, and then worse, I forgot about it." Tadahisa stared at Namiyo.

Namiyo wasn't surprised; there were rumours about Tadahisa – addiction issues and rounds of rehab visits, although he was apparently doing fine now.

"I need someone to create something truly wonderful for it. Would you at least consider my proposal?"

Namiyo nodded and watched Tadahisa carefully pull out the long black silk wrapped object and lay it on the low table. By the shape, Namiyo knew this would be the sword. Tadahisa removed another long box, placed it next to the wrapped sword and carefully lifted the lid so the curved cream-coloured item was revealed, sitting among the crimson tissue paper.

Namiyo leaned across and examined what was in there; he tenderly pulled it out and ran his fingers over the contours. He took it over to the window and held it up under the light, twisting it around so he could see it clearly. He turned and looked at Tadahisa.

"This is part of a mammoth tusk," he said.

"It's legal," Tadahisa said. "I have the documentation."

"From Siberia?"

Tadahisa nodded.

Namiyo walked back, placed it back on the tissue paper inside the box and looked at Tadahisa. "What is it you want me to do with it?"

"Carve a dragon tsuka."

Namiyo stared at the other man until he became uncomfortable and lowered his eyes.

"Please, this is important to me. Whatever you want to charge I'll pay and how you want to carve it is up to you. I just need someone who will be discreet and will carve something special. I know that man is you," Tadahisa said.

Namiyo hesitated; "how much are you willing to pay?"

Tadahisa replied, "whatever you ask."

Namiyo stood up and walked over to the windows, the storm was closer now; there were rain splatters appearing on the dark concrete pavers.

"Leave it here. I'll let you know in a few days and I'll send you some rough sketches." He didn't turn around, he stood watching the rain clouds open up, pouring water over the deck, a curtain of black water that obliterated everything, the deluge so loud he couldn't hear the other man stand and walk away.

***

He repacked the two items in their bag and took it to his studio; he unpacked the sword, a wonderful piece of craftsmanship, he ran his fingers carefully across the polished steel, his own grandfather had been a master sword-maker, and he could tell that this piece was exquisite. Namiyo pulled out the mammoth tusk and laid it next to the sword. There was something very compelling about this object, although he hadn't worked with a tusk before, he knew he had the skills to do this. He sat for a long while with his eyes closed, feeling the texture of the rough ivory, feeling the strength held within its carbon fibres. It was thousands of years old, and he wondered about its long story of burial beneath the icy wastelands. He awoke to discover he had fallen asleep, his face against this enormous tooth; he had been dreaming, but the images were elusive and ephemeral, dissipating into the shadows.

The storm had passed, and he opened the door and walked into a clear night, the sky far above partially obscured by the forest of bamboo that covered this part of his family's estate. The scent of the wet earth and leaves revived him, the gentle swishing and rustling, the creaking and knocking of the stalks against each other, these were some of his favourite sounds, and why he chose to have his bedroom and studio here. He felt a feline shape against his calves, he leaned down and let his fingers drift into that long fur, she pressed into his body more. He picked her up; so black she was indistinguishable from the night, except for those yellow eyes.

"What have you been doing, my Mizuki?" he whispered, "hunting for frogs, is that what you are doing?"

He held her close so her face was pressed against his cheek; she purred, her face so warm, so alive unlike the long dead object he had been resting his face against before. A shiver ran along his entire body – starting at his head and moving down along his torso and arms. Momentarily Mizuki stopped purring and a small miaow came out.

"You feel it too, don't you?" he whispered. This moment felt like a separating line, carving off the Namiyo of today and the Namiyo that had emerged to stand here. Two Namiyos, for a brief moment together, and then splintered, one dissolving into the past and one rising up within him, unfurling out. There was an ominous quality to it yet also an inevitable, unavoidable aspect that he would just need to accept and incorporate.

He carried Mizuki in, found a sachet for her among his supplies and watched as she happily ate from her bowl. He went to bed and dreamed big thundering dreams under a sky where the constellations moved differently from how they did now.

He drew some sketches and sent them off to Tadahisa saying that one of them would be the one he would carve; he didn't give the man a choice because the choice was neither of theirs. Once he began he would know which of the dragons wished to embody itself within this new home. And which the tusk would accept. It was symbiotic; between them the mystery would be awakened and revealed.

He rang his fiancé, Kimiko, and told her he would be working for at least a week or so.

She laughed as she said, "Yes, that is why I pulled the Hermit card last night; you must enter your dark cave and do what you must do. I will immerse myself in what I need to do."

***

Day and night wove together; he worked and slept, carving the tusk, carving the dragon, carving himself. The fire of the fever came over him, bringing the dreams and the hallucinations. Or was it around the other way? Namiyo walked between the worlds. Sometimes he was a mammoth, a huge beast that stomped across the plains, shaking the earth with its immensity. Sometimes he was a man, a hunter and spear-maker of his tribe, carving the tools they needed to bring down the huge animals they hunted, honing them to a deadly sharpness. He felt the sun shining on his back as he bent over the rock shards meticulously working. Sometimes it was the flames of the fire on his face as he carved a miniature deer from an antler. Sometimes it was the heat rising from his own body as he stared into the eye of the dragon that was appearing out of the ivory.

Some nights he burned like a comet as he rode on the backs of enormous dragons that wheeled through the air. Or his skin was drenched in the water of enchanted lakes as the dragons plunged into the endless depths. Other nights he lay deathly cold in the underworld of the earth, within the permafrost, the ice that burned his skin, the intense coldness that ached in his bones. Far above him the seasons turned, the moon and the sun danced their dance, but below there was a death within life within death stasis of just being suspended within time.

As the fever grew stronger, the moments of lucidity grew less. The dragon was appearing; nearly all was complete, he only needed to hold on a little longer but it was so hard. Namiyo carved almost as though he were blind as his mind took him deeper into the visions that had become omens of a future that was rapidly barrelling towards him, towards them all. Volcanoes erupting along the fault lines, many had been dormant for a thousand years but were now waking and erupting with a deep anger. Earthquakes rupturing the earth, shaking and moving, and calling to the tsunamis rising out of the depths like watery dragons being released. Firestorms burning through the forests, obscuring the sun and creating a hellish environment where nothing could survive. The smoke so thick and huge it drifted across hundreds of miles, turning cities into twilight zones, where the air was almost unbreathable, and the birds stopped singing. Storms, hurricanes, and cyclones circling this beautiful planet, their destructive power immense. As the ferocity of their winds and the tides that were unleashed, the waterfalls that moved in arcs across the heavens and the relentlessness of the flooding carved new dragons onto the landscape.

And the microscopic, the tiny almost invisible contagions rising up from the melting permafrosts; the glaciers, the thawing of long dead and buried carcasses from the era when giants roamed the world: the mammoths and mastodons, the large feline predators like *smilodon*, the sabre-toothed cats, and the immense ice bears. Microbes and viruses drifted up into the air, hitching rides on the warm bodies of migrating birds that circumnavigated the earth, falling down upon new fertile fields, new warm bodies, new nests to propagate themselves. New plagues that would rise up and add their melody to the song of destruction that Earth was singing. Namiyo laughed softly at that, knowing that within the core of his body one such contagion had nestled and was creating an inner firestorm, a fight to the death, from which he would either rise up or return to the cold deep earth.

***

It was Kimiko and his mother who found him lying on the floor, still holding one of his tools in his clenched fist. Kimiko had gone to visit him, concerned by his lack of communication. Mizuki had run in beside them and was now on his worktable hissing at the air. Together they managed to carry Namiyo to his bed. His clothes drenched wet with the fever. Soon the doctors came with their gloves, gowns, and facemasks and their worried advice and frowns, telling Kimiko and Aoi that a new virus was circling the globe, a new pandemic had emerged.

"Is this what my son has?" Aoi demanded sharply, her emotions causing her to speak more harshly that she would normally.

"We don't know," the senior doctor replied, anxiety in his eyes wary of causing offence to one of the oldest and wealthiest families in Japan. "But please, you are to quarantine at home until further notice. One of us will come back daily to check on your son's progress and also make sure that this illness hasn't spread to any of you."

Kimiko sat beside Namiyo and cared for him, gently washing his body, and cleaning the sheets. She squeezed drops of water into his mouth as his moaned. She spoke to him softly, telling him stories of her childhood and of long forgotten dreams. Mizuki curled up beside him as well, her purrs filling the air like some healing frequency.

It was a week before he regained consciousness and the fever finally broke. Kimiko spooned miso broth into his mouth while he lay weak and exhausted on the bed. No other member of the family or any servants became sick. When Namiyo was strong enough to walk, she led him to a long couch that she had pulled out into the grove of bamboo; it was here the morning sun shone warmly onto him as he lay among the cushions. She sat beside him in another chair, leaving at intervals to bring rice dishes that they shared. They didn't speak much; the sound of the bamboo stalks swaying in the wind was as healing as the nutrients in the food.

One afternoon she walked into his studio, opening the windows to let the fresh air blow through, she stood beside the table and stared at the cream dragon that he had carved, the sinewy shape of its body as it wove around and along the sword handle. She picked it up, the eyes staring at her as though they could actually see her. She noticed that at the very end of the tail, it curled and became a miniature mammoth nestled in those coils. She smiled at that.

"Please put it down," his voice was loud and made her start.

"Of course," she replied, "I understand, I was very gentle." She placed it down carefully.

Namiyo's eyes were huge in his thin face, his cheekbones looking as carved as flesh could look, harsh angles within the paleness of his skin. Fear had grasped his throat so tightly he couldn't speak. *No*, he wanted to say, *no it is not you that I fear will damage the dragon, it is what lies within the dragon that I fear will harm you.*

He walked towards her and clasped her hands, leading her outside to the tap where he let the chilly water pour over both their hands until his hands were so cold that he could barely feel them, and he knew she must be feeling it too. Yet, she did not flinch. He led her over to a spot where a large boulder was sunlit, and they placed their icy hands on the warm stone.

The fear had subsided now, and Namiyo knew that it was irrational; if she was going to get sick, she would've already, and she had been beside him for almost three weeks, breathing in his breaths as she cared for him.

"I haven't properly thanked you for everything you did for me while I was sick. You truly went beyond what anyone would've expected you to do. I don't know how I will ever repay you," he said, staring into her eyes.

"I don't need thanks. The thanks are in you being alive." She smiled, but her lovely eyes were sad.

She knows, he thought, *somehow, she knows everything.*

Even though the decision has only just coalesced in his mind, or perhaps the decision had been made long ago, and he had only just become aware of it. Namiyo knew that during the fever, the man he was to become had incorporated itself fully within his bones and cells. It was going to take a while before he would be able to put all that in action, but his mind was already working on the logistics of it and what that would mean.

Chapter Ten

Here, said she,
Is your card, the drowned Phoenician Sailor,
(Those are pearls that were his eyes. Look!)
Here is Belladonna, the Lady of the Rocks,
The lady of situations.

T S Eliot

The Present

Halo stood in a garden of contorted shapes, the light shone down on a bed of raked sand and it reflected back like from a luminous mirror. He could smell a sharp pine odour. He walked carefully on the path of cut rock and up onto the verandah and into the room; the floors were polished wood, a golden-brown hue, the panelled walls were made from translucent rice paper screens. Lanterns wavered from the ceiling and gave out a rich, smoky fragrance. A layer of folded quilts lay in a tidy pile on the floor.

He approached and kneeled down. A young girl lay sleeping, her dark hair partly obscured one side of her face, her lips were smiling. The shadows from the lantern light made it hard to discern her face. Halo felt it was Raven, but he wasn't sure. There was something about the slant of her cheekbones that reminded him of Jinja. He reached over to brush aside her hair but stopped when he heard the footsteps.

He looked at the figure approaching. The man was very tall; he was wearing a kimono of indigo blue. The man sat down on some cushions that were arranged neatly on the floor and beckoned Halo to join him. The man's countenance was in shadow; as though he willed the darkness to cover him.

"Welcome," the stranger spoke in a voice that was icy like glacial rivers. "I must congratulate you. Your emotions are very strong, they are like deep dangerous waters; they appear calm and navigable but once you are in their depths it is very easy to drown. And drowning can be very pleasurable."

He leaned forward. Now his face was out of the shadows and Halo could see him. His hair was short and an uncommon white with a sheen that reminded Halo of pearls; his skin was also extremely light, and the bones underneath seemed to pierce the skin with fragile edges, so he appeared to be cut from some strange glass like substance. His eyes were his most consuming aspect; they were like violet flames. There was a large sliver of black crystal that hung like a dagger around his neck. It had a heavy malevolent aura to it.

"I enjoy competition. Do you?"

"Depends what game we're playing," Halo replied warily.

"You and I are the same. Underneath. You realise that?"

"I don't think so."

"Ah, but we are. You won't admit to it. If you would only surrender to yourself – to what you truly are – otherwise, the game is won before it has been played."

"What game?"

The stranger smiled and looked around the room before saying; "the Japanese are most interesting. Wouldn't you agree? I feel a kinship to them. You do too. I enjoy their subterfuge, they have developed secrecy into an art, their faces, their tone of voice betray nothing. A bland controlled exterior that hides a seething network of, dare I say, excessiveness. Did you know that the dead in Japan have links to the living that are so strong they must be severed in special ceremonies that last forty-nine days? Then they must be further appeased yearly just in case they return as vengeful spirits bent on destruction. As Soul Devourers."

The stranger parted his lips, his teeth glinted in the light. He was still, as though waiting on an answer before continuing.

"Have you ever wondered why Japan has so many earthquakes? It has nothing to do with their geology; it's a spiritual dimension. All that containment, all those dreams bound and constrained like bonsai. It must be let loose occasionally, and when it blows, my friend, you would not begin to comprehend the intricate violence of their dream tapestries: the darkness, the richness, and the insaneness of their nightmares. I was there during a particularly devastating one, a tsunami formed, a hundred miles off the coast and swept in like the watery hand of God. The creatures that rode that wave were more grotesque than any monk of the inquisition could have dreamed up, and more beautiful than any form alive. Nightmares, shadows, demons given a body."

There was rustling and Halo looked over at the sleeping girl. She had moved and now her face was directly in the lamp's glow.

"You know where we are? You've been here before." Halo heard the words as he looked at the girl's features.

It was Jinja, her heart shaped face, sleeping and tranquil.

"Did you enjoy your little tryst?" the stranger moved out of the shadows, the face was now Takiyo's. "Did you enjoy my sister? Did you enjoy her kisses? Did you enjoy her touch? Was she a good geisha girl? Did she pleasure you?"

Takiyo's smile made his skin stretch like fine brown leather.

"Was she worth it? Was it worth her death?"

Takiyo jumped to his feet. He was all grace and lightness, he covered the distance to the bed with one leap as though he were a jaguar and Jinja was the prey. He grabbed her by the hair and pulled her off the bed. Her eyes opened in horror and pain. Takiyo pulled out a thin sword from inside his kimono and slit her throat in one swift flow. There was no blood; just emptiness where her body had been. Takiyo swirled around in a flurry of midnight-blue material. Jinja was no longer. In her place a whirlwind of petals scattered to the ground. The stranger laughed. He was seated back where he had been.

"Life is an illusion. Death even more so. All of reality is fragmented, only a mirage contains a glimmer of truth and that is too insubstantial to really hold, to really perceive."

"What about a mirror?" Halo hissed.

"Oh, very good. I am impressed, really," the stranger smiled intimately. "You've played this game before. But you are forgetting one thing; to see into a mirror, one needs light. A mirror is useless when one is in darkness. So, this is the important part. And I am being more then generous," his voice had taken on the texture of honey.

"If you intend to use the mirror, you must not use it in the dark," he smiled. His eyes were intense; almost like fire and they burned into Halo's. His voice was low like a whisper of an approaching storm; "I know your darkest dreams. I know your fears. I know your secrets and your shadows; I know what is buried so deep you could not find them. But I could. I could dredge them up. I could make them real again. You would not like that." The stranger's voice swelled around Halo like a bulging river that had broken its banks.

"Leave what belongs to me, leave what doesn't concern you alone. She is mine," the voice grew into a waterfall that roared over and into and through him, pushing him under into a spinning maelstrom. "You couldn't save her last time, you won't this time."

"When was it when we last met? When? Where?" Halo shouted as he fought the gruelling current. It momentarily subsided.

"Perhaps I shall tell you – I feel like making the game more interesting. Six hundred years ago, your pride was your downfall. She was your charge, your responsibility; all you had to do was bring her home safe. Which, in those days, was not the easiest of tasks I will admit. But, you were ever the courageous one, you on your battle horse, your shiny armour, your sword at the ready; the strong, resourceful knight, a crusader veteran, trusted by the king to escort his only daughter home. And she was so lovely, so innocent, and the path home was through the forest – the almost-impenetrable forest that covered half the world. Too many trees, too many beasts; some real, some imaginary, and always so dark the path was, and so long. But you thought you could have it all – the maiden and the beast – and what a hero you would be. Instead you lost them both and your penance was death." The stranger laughed.

"And before?" Halo asked, his voice steady as some glimmer of past truths held him upright.

"You ask too much. You want too much."

"Tell me. Scared? Is that it? Too scared to tell me? Maybe I'll defeat you this time," Halo laughed although fear griped his stomach.

"Scared of you? Insignificant crawling beetle that you are – I don't think so," the stranger stared at Halo disdainfully. He licked his lips; his teeth looked sharp.

"One thousand years ago was the first time. Just before what you call a millennium. All those fears, all those hopes, a smorgasbord of apocalypses and messiahs. Always makes my time more rewarding. It was on this mountain where we met, maybe even this spot. She was your sister, you were younger than her. You were the child destined for the monastery, for you had the sight and you could see what others couldn't. You knew about the coming tsunami, you felt it building along the fault lines of humanities mind, but you were mute. The bitter irony of it."

The stranger paused, Halo looked at his face partially hidden by the barren branches that swirled out of the vase on the low table; these twisted remnants of a once living thing.

"It was hard. Harder than I expected; you had the stubbornness, the resilience of a child. And she loved you so, her little brother of no voice, loved you to the point of selflessness. She died to save you. She gave herself in return that you would live. That was the bargain. And you became the holy man that was your destiny. Helping to unite Shinto with Buddhism, creating something unique. It was your destiny, but the payment was rather severe wouldn't you say?"

"I don't believe any of this."

"Your choice. It matters little to me what you chose to believe or disbelieve."

The stranger leaned back, his face once more in shadow.

"But you always lose. You lost then as a child and later, as a man. And now you are something in-between."

"Who are you?"

"Your adversary," those unearthly eyes bored into Halo's.

"What are you?"

The stranger laughed again, amused. "Think about it. Dredge up some of those long-dead memories. Make it harder for me if you can; if you dare," he paused for a moment, and gave an exaggerated sigh. "It would be diverting to have a challenge. Even a small one would amuse me."

Halo looked around the room, imprinting it on his memory; he was feeling weak. He knew he must remember this place, this conversation. If he didn't, he would lose again. Somehow this was terribly important.

"She is mine. Leave her to me. If you come between us then death will be more pleasurable than what I have in store for you. You cannot win."

Halo screamed as he fell through a vortex of stars and planets, with the stranger's laughter swirling around him like a comet heading for the sun.

***

He found himself on the floor, lying on the polished boards, had he fallen from his chair? His computer had gone into sleep mode. He looked at the kaleidoscope of patterns swirling on the glass screen that took up part of the wall. He tried to remember what he had been doing. He had been trawling the web. Had he tumbled into the slipstream? Or had he deliberately chosen to go there? Had he fallen asleep? Was this a dream or something else entirely?

Chapter Eleven

You have always frightened me,
Hermes the unknown, you who help me.
You make me the peer of Midas,
The saddest of all alchemists;
Through you I change gold to iron
And make of paradise a hell.

Charles Baudelaire

Raven fingered the white dress; it was made of silk and was very delicate. She pulled it over her head and let it flow down her body. The bodice was tight fitting and intricately embroidered, from the waist the garment floated to her ankles in a mass of light airy fabric. She had taken it from one of the forgotten hordes in the huge attic; merchandise that had been scammed from online and occasionally got left behind. It was the perfect dress to wear when going to meet your unicorn.

She laughed, it was all so unreal. Who was Ceriful? He claimed to have come from beyond the veil. He was lost, looking for something. What, she hadn't been able to ascertain. She felt he may have slipped out into this reality like those other creatures she could see, but they were malevolent, he wasn't. There was a kindness, and sensitivity within him. He was beautiful too. Unearthly. Last time, he had allowed her to climb on his back and they galloped through the desolate ruins, it had been a wonderful experience. She had felt so happy – so connected. When she was with him, she didn't feel alone anymore.

She left her room and bolted the door. She was very territorial, this was her space, and no one was going to get in. She descended the stairs to the huge living area that took over the whole lower floor. She said hello to some of the occupants she knew and ignored those she didn't. It was reasonably quiet today, most people were probably working away inside the left wing of the mansion where all the electronics were kept, and the extra generators needed to power the Nexus were housed. She found Aurora outside in the shady courtyard; she was sitting in the rocking chair holding a sleeping baby, which had arrived a few weeks ago. It was a chubby cheeked thing and sort of cute.

Raven had been with Aurora for seven years, Aurora was like an older sister; she kept some of the more sleazy carnies away and stood up against the ones that came in and demanded too much of Raven. One time when Raven had been trawling the Web for over forty-eight hours straight, Aurora had come in, punched the overseer out and pulled Raven, half unconscious, out of the Nexus. After that she kept strict time calls on Raven. Raven was the best PilotFish the Carnies had; she could move so silently through the interface, attaching tiny fishnets to the endless streams of code that flowed through. Each were capable of pulling down micro seeds of pelf, which when added up as a total, was a lot of coinage. Yet it was so cleverly hidden as micro percentages, they usually didn't ping any warnings.

She leaned over and told Aurora she was going out for a while and wouldn't be home till late.

"Who are you meeting dressed like that? Is it a boy?" Aurora asked, "or a girl? I do hope it's someone special?"

Raven just smiled.

The sun was a burning disk, so she kept to the shadowed side of the road and took the back streets and the forgotten alleys reaching the Ghostlands within a short space of time. The heat seemed more intense here; the grass was dead, the earth cracked, all that lived here were lizards and swarms of grasshoppers that cast a baleful eye on any intruder.

She was almost at her destination when she heard footsteps. She turned around. He was older than her, big in a burly sort of way. His face was square and he had large fleshy lips and small eyes. His head was shaved.

"What you doing round here?" he broke the silence with a voice that was guttural.

She wanted to ignore him and keep walking, but that would mean turning her back on him, not a good idea, she knew.

"That's a real pretty dress," he said casually eyeing her. "A pretty dress for a pretty girl."

He stepped forward, she moved back. He grinned at her.

"Now, why would you be here? What would make a nice girl like you come to a desolate place like this?"

Raven inched another step away.

"Come to meet your lover-boy maybe?"

Raven moved back, and found she was against a wall. He advanced so fast she had no time to react. He pushed her hard against the wall, his hands pining her at her shoulders, his mouth on hers; the fleshy lips hot and blubbery, his tongue forcing its way through her clenched teeth.

He pulled away and she screamed, he slapped her and covered her mouth with his hand.

"Now why'd you do that? We were having such a good time, and you had to go and spoil it."

With his free hand he roughly began to fondle her breasts. She kicked her legs, tried to move but his heavy body had her pinned against the wall. He continued with his grotesque caress.

"Now, let's have a look at what you been hiding under there," he said as he hauled her dress up above her knees. She felt his hands roughly pushing her thighs apart. She felt his fingers push against the fabric of her underpants. She stared at him, trying to work out how to bite him, but his big hands were immovable. Her head ached with the pressure of being held.

Then, she felt him move jerkily against her and his face looked suddenly bewildered – shocked. A tiny bubble of pinkish saliva formed at his mouth. His hands were less powerful; she pushed them away. She saw a sliver of black jutting out of his chest. She watched in horror as the pointed blade retracted and blood came gushing out. He swayed and fell backward. The man looked up at her with sightless eyes as a pool of liquid spread out, soaking the parched earth.

Raven looked at Ceriful. His long, black horn was coated with slimy body fluids, and blood dripped off the point, marking his white coat and trickling down his silky mane. He stamped his hooves and shook his head; drops of blood splayed from his horn and sprayed the ground and his legs. His eyes were now black and electric; she could feel the surges of power that seemed to be gathering.

"Go!" He screamed into her mind. "Go! Leave now!"

She grabbed her bag and ran. She was even more scared than before. For a split moment as Ceriful had screamed she had seen and felt the state of his mind. There was immense darkness and savagery, it was primitive and alien, and contained something she did not want to comprehend.

"Don't come back. I will let you know when it is safe."

As she ran, she knew that he meant safe from him. She knew with a dreadful certainty that if she had stayed, he might not have been able to stop himself from impaling her with his cold ebony horn. Piercing and killing her.

Eventually she stopped running. She could hardly breathe and the sweat was streaming out of her body. She saw a tram rattling towards her and clambered on board. The conductor approached her, and she paid the money and received a ticket. It was very expensive; it must be one of the historic tourist trams she thought. Soon the tram was rattling down the corridors of the city, the tall buildings cast shadows, and from one of the high ledges she observed the gargoyles leaning over the edge, their grotesque faces peering out at the people scurrying below. The tram turned a corner, and her vision was taken up by mirrored glass that rammed up into the sky, an impossible distance. The tram filled with people, so many that some were standing in the walkways or jammed up against the doors. The tram rattled on. It crossed the river and headed out on a raised platform. It gathered speed like some beast let loose. The city receded in the distance.

"This is the last stop, honey." The tram conductor's lilting voice broke through Raven's haze.

She left the tram and followed the people. She walked down the boulevard. The palms swayed in the slight breeze, and she could see the glint of water, the bay spread out to the horizon, its pale blue blending into the raw heat blue of the sky. The high rise apartment blocks, their dirty cream paint peeling away like sunburn on skin, sat next to the brand new hotels with their street level bars overflowing with long-legged girls and muscle-armed boys. Dogs sniffed around the gutters. A group of men stood on a corner singing ancient war songs in a lost language that was sadly melodious and haunting. The brawny singers smiled as they sang. Raven sensed in the rhythm undertows of destruction and hostility, a battle cry to bloodshed and glory and death. The song made Raven's mind fill with dark thoughts, blood as black as ink swirled in whirlpools and threatened to pull her into its maelstrom. She crossed the road.

Inside the amusement park the screams from the roller-coaster as it jolted precariously over the man-made mountains made her flinch, the music from some of the rides made her nauseous. She walked away and then she was at the carousel, the painted horses moving up and down, their kohl rimmed eyes staring endlessly out. Raven stood and watched them, deriving a strange sort of peace from their gentle prancing and their familiar bodies. She wanted to step up and climb onto one of the brightly coloured steeds; she wanted to rest her forehead against their rippling manes plaited with golden and red ribbons.

Red ribbons against their cream coats.

Red on white.

Blood red on ivory white. The colours flashed into her mind, and she felt sickened and stumbled away from the bright lights and the organ music.

She hardly noticed as she walked past the crazy mirrors, her reflection turning from squat and wide, to tall and insect-thin. She strode past the house of horrors with its comic-like representations of ghosts, ghouls, and vampires. Kids pushed past her, groups of girls postured in front of groups of boys who were showing their skill at shooting slow moving plastic ducks. She found the atmosphere claustrophobic, the voices screeching, the smell of humanity seared her nostrils, the sweat of armpits, the cooling scent of suntan lotion, the salty sea fragrance, the cheap cologne, the hot cinnamon donuts, and the cigarette smoke.

She made her way back to the entrance where she bought a can of carbonated water. Under the huge gaping mouth that covered the gateway she stopped and drank the ice cold drink. She was starting to feel better. Then she saw him; he stood out from the crowd as though a spotlight was on him.

"We have to stop meeting like this," Halo said.

Chapter Twelve

Oh Love! How perfect is thy mystic art,
How self-deceitful is the sagest part
Of mortals whom thy lure hath led along—
The precipice she stood on was immense,
So was her creed in her own innocence.

Lord Byron

"**W**hat are you doing here?" she asked.

"I had a drink with a friend who lives nearby."

"What are you doing now?" her expression sad.

"Nothing," Halo said. "What about you?"

She surprised him when she said, "nothing."

He touched her arm; she pulled away slightly and then relaxed. He whispered; "so, let's you and I do nothing together."

"Do you want to go in?" he pointed towards the amusement park. She shook her head. "Let's go down to the beach then."

He took her hand and squeezed it. They walked across the road and over the lawn, past the ice-cream sellers and the hot dog stands. His hand was warm and soft, and she felt strangely safe and comforted.

They sat on the sand, the sun was low on the horizon, partly obscured by feathery clouds, coloured silver and tinged with rose. A slight breeze blew off the bay and alleviated the stifling heat. The beach was still crowded; people were swimming in the calm waters, and others were lazing on their beach towels. Raven sat cross legged, her hands played with the sand in front of her, abstract sandcastles formed and reformed as she dug her fingers into the sand. Halo watched her fingers playing with the grains, there was a sensual quality to the way her hands caressed the granules, the whiteness slipping through those long fingers, and falling silently back down onto the beach.

She looked out at the horizon; the sun had sunk lower and she could just see the enormous steel barriers that held back the real sea, that maelstrom of wild and raging waves that would destroy and shatter all of this if ever released. She remembered that this place had been rebuilt – piece-by-piece – some of it using the original material, further inland where an artificial bay had been created. They had carefully reconstructed this district, so it was virtually the same as the original. Aurora said people were nostalgic – that they yearned for times that were no longer, even if those times realistically hadn't been that pleasant.

She looked at Halo. His eyes are too blue, Raven was thinking, they are like the sky, too raw, too scorching.

Her eyes are too sad, Halo thought, misty grey like rain, falling, falling soundlessly.

"What now little girl?" he asked.

She looked over at the shoreline. There were black creatures swaggering through the shallows, shadowy skeleton thin creatures with elongated arms and legs and small heads shrouded with black veils. Four of them, Raven counted, they strutted through the water, sidestepping the children playing there. Sending up small splashes of water as they moved. No one else could see them Raven knew, because if they did, they would not be acting so blithely. The creatures moved silently, their heads swaying from side to side. One of them turned and she saw its face. No eyes and a large, cavernous mouth, yet she knew it saw her.

"I want to go somewhere. Somewhere quiet, away from everyone. Somewhere safe."

"Safe from what?"

"Just safe."

Halo stood up and reached down and took her hand; "let's go."

He pulled her up.

"Where?" she whispered.

"Somewhere safe," Halo whispered back.

He led her to where his pod was parked. An ambulance howled past, its siren shattering the happy sounds of the seashore, sending a flock of pigeons into panic. Raven stumbled as though the sound was concrete and had formed irregular bumps in the pavement. A young child went running by, she was carrying an ice-cream cone, the top wobbled and fell onto the pavement, a deep raspberry shade of goo melted on the hot pavement and ran in rivulets of garish red. Raven stared at it; the buzzing in her head was so intense she thought her brain might explode.

"What's wrong?" Halo's voice was very distant.

Raven looked around her, the swaying palm trees, the flock of birds winging across the sky, the old tower with its bleached paintwork, the sky that was turning pale as though the blue was leaking away. Now it was the colour of bone and everything else as well, the trees were no longer green but fading into black, and the birds were shadowy scars on a fading negative. Halo caught her as she fell. She lay limp in his arms.

***

She awoke in an unfamiliar room; the windows were open letting in a cool breeze. He was standing in the doorway.

"How are you?"

Her eyes did not leave his face.

"How are you feeling?" he asked the question again.

"Where am I?"

"You're at my place. I brought you here after you fainted."

"I fainted?"

"Well, it looked like that to me."

Raven slowly sat up, "could I have a shower?"

Halo showed her to the bathroom and handed her a towel.

"Do you like pizza? I thought I'd order some food."

"Yes, thank you." Raven held the towel in a fierce grip, with her other hand she held on to the rail. The floor seemed to be swaying gently.

"Are you sure you are all right?" Halo asked, concerned.

Raven nodded. Halo shut the door and left her to shower. She emerged a little later, her hair was still wet, she had combed it back off her face and it covered her head like a shiny damp cap. Her eyes were very bright. She came and sat at the dining table. Halo sat across from her.

"Feeling better?"

"Mm. Feel really good," her eyes sparkled.

"Pizza shouldn't be long now. Would you like a drink?"

Raven looked at Halo with a strange smile on her face.

"What is it?" Halo asked.

"It's my birthday."

"Happy Birthday. Well, since it's your birthday we should have something special to drink. Champagne?"

"Champagne?" she repeated. "I've never had champagne."

"Even better," he walked to the kitchen and pulled out a chilled bottle.

He searched for some champagne flutes, and grabbed a couple of candlesticks. Might as well make it really special. He handed her one of the delicate flutes. She ran her fingers down the fragile glass, lightly tapping the rim, it tinkled and she laughed with pleasure. He forced the cork out, it exploded and hit the ceiling, then bounced back, just missing the glasses. The liquid was golden.

He lifted his glass. "To you, happy birthday."

She picked up her flute, gazed at the bubbles frothing in the liquid, she took a sip and giggled.

"Are you going to tell me how old you are today?"

She looked at the candle flame with a wistful expression on her face.

"Sixteen," she answered. "Is that too young?"

"For what?" he asked.

"For anything." She whispered.

He moved the candles to one side and leaned over the table. He felt the hard wooden edge dig into his ribs, and he could almost see his reflection in the polished wood. He kissed her very gently, very softly. Her lips were warm, and he could taste traces of the wine. They gazed at each other.

The intercom buzzed.

"That'll be the pizza," Halo said.

They ate, drank, talked, and laughed. Halo put some music on, part Caribbean, part Latino. The rhythm was infectious, but the tone was undercut with a sad melancholy edge. The candles were flickering from wafts of air that were coming through the open French doors. The night was balmy. Halo went to the fridge and pulled out a second bottle. He felt light-headed, almost drunk.

Raven was wandering around the room looking at the framed pictures. The exploding cork made her turn around. He filled both their glasses, handing her one. She was very focused on one of the paintings; black brushstrokes on a creamy parchment. It was a bird on a bamboo stalk.

"One of my mother's," he acknowledged.

"It's very . . ." she struggled to find the words.

"Japanese," he filled in the sentence.

"Yes."

"She learned to paint like that when we were in Japan."

"When was that?" Raven asked.

"Two years ago."

"What was it like?"

"Strange. Exciting. Lonely." That just about summed it up, he thought.

"Does she still paint?" Raven asked.

"Yeah. It's her passion."

"Where are your parents now?"

"In New Hong Kong. My father is working on a project that will help them combat the pollution levels. Well, that's the plan."

"What's it like to live in a nice place like this? I mean it's so stylish."

Halo shrugged.

"We haven't always lived in homes as nice as this. We've lived in some pretty out-there places too. I was born in a commune. Up in the far north. My parents were Eco Hippies, they had dropped off the grid. Everything we had was handmade or bartered, and our power came from renewable energy. It was a great childhood really; we got to bathe in the streams and grow stuff and run through the jungle pretending we were the last people on earth. But, it was hard too. We didn't have much that was high-tech at all, and what we did was solar powered and not always reliable. My father basically perfected the salt water powered engine for pods; they existed before, but they were very expensive, and he created a small, highly efficient cell that harnessed the electricity. His brother was a patents lawyer, which meant that he wasn't going to get ripped off. We ended up moving to Europa where he worked on it with a German company, and a new phase of our life began."

"I hadn't meant to imply anything," Raven said defensively.

"I know," he replied. He wanted to say more – he knew how different her lifestyle was from his. "Shall we dance?" he asked, took her by the hand, and led her to the middle of the room.

As they danced, she put her arms around his neck, tilted her head back and laughed. Her throat was an alabaster white, and his gaze was drawn to the tiny pulse near the side of her neck. It was mesmerising; it beat against her skin like a fragile imprisoned moth and he could almost see it under the surface – tiny and intricate the wings were beating, beating, beating. She kissed him; it was a seductive kiss, her tongue fluttered against his mouth, her lips bruising his with the intensity. His hand ran down her back and he could feel the heat from her skin through the light cotton fabric of her dress.

Halo felt one of her hands against his shirt undoing the buttons. She was deft and quick – she pulled the fabric free, and her hands were caressing his chest. He involuntarily moaned. They were both breathing quickly, her lips were fuller then normal; the colour had deepened to crimson.

They had stopped dancing; she reached down to the hem of her dress and gathered up the material, moving it over her body, she lifted her arms, and he pulled the garment free. She stood in front of him wearing only her white bra and pants. Raven kissed him and he pulled her almost-naked body against him. She was so hot, and her skin seemed to scorch him where her naked skin touched his. He rubbed himself against her, the jeans rough and hard against her soft burning skin. His tongue was inside her mouth.

Halo hesitated; he still held her as he felt the candles flicker as a cold breeze swirled through the open doors, and her body which was hard and firm against his, suddenly went soft and loose. He caught her as she fell. He carried her to the couch and lay her down. He was worried now; she had fainted twice in a matter of hours. He could still feel the imprint of her body against his; feel the taste of her mouth.

He sat down next to her and stroked her hair tenderly. Was it drugs? Not likely. She had always been anti-chemical. Was she unwell? She didn't look sick. He went to his bedroom and pulled the sheet off the bed and covered her with it.

Perhaps it was for the best, he thought, *she was so young; sixteen!*

What had he been thinking? He had been reacting, not thinking, and although he was only two years older, she had a vulnerability – an innocence that he had always been conscious of. Despite her being a Carnie, she had an ethereal quality; otherworldly almost. It was probably what had most attracted him in the beginning. That along with the take-no-prisoners way she played Go.

Chapter Thirteen

The Japanese Festival of the Dead is held in July. During this time the spirits of the dead are welcomed back into their former homes, offered meals and allowed to wander through the rooms and gardens. Three days later the spirits are released to return to the underworld. Spirits who have no relatives are honoured by little boats bearing paper lanterns and are set afloat on the Tide of Returning Ghosts, to drift out to sea.

Halo knew he was going to go in. He had been resisting it for so long, it was like an irresistible thread that drew him, he felt himself fall and then he was floating in the silver slipstream with an aurora flashing above him. He sensed he wasn't alone; strange, tiny creatures like dragonflies flittered about, they were a translucent silver and their wings moved so fast that it was like trying to watch lightning. There was music too, a choir, faint, unearthly and haunting, the song seemed to flow around him and every few beats it would crash over him, like some vibratory wave surging.

What is this place? he thought, as he let the current take him.

The flickering of the light was hypnotic, one of the dragonflies had landed on his finger, she was like some delicate fairy, her exquisite feminine body ended in a serpentine whip shape. Jewels of sapphire and emerald glittered on her skin. She smiled at him; showing him her teeth, which were filed to long thin points. She bit him and the slipstream turned to scarlet. All around blood red sea serpents twisted and undulated; and swimming between them were mermaids, black skinned with tails like obsidian flakes, and they sparkled like a sky of dark stars. He could feel himself fading, turning; he spun around slowly in a spiral of luminescence, and he knew that he might never break from this downward helix.

Then she was there, holding him, pulling him from the black hole that was dragging him away. Her hands were like a spiral galaxy as she pulled him back into the slipstream; above her a super nova was about to explode. White light slashed with red, like a terrible eye spun beyond her. She held him and pulled him out.

Halo awoke, his body covered in sweat. He and Raven were both on the floor. He felt like he had been thrown on some alien shore where nothing was as it appeared.

"You were there?" he gasped.

He felt ill, there was a creeping sensation that was climbing up his spine and clutching into his neck, its grip was tight and uncompromising; he felt the sweat break out on his forehead. There was a roaring in his ears like a massive waterfall, and he felt icy cold as the grip on his neck tightened and his stomach heaved. He took a deep breath and the spasm passed.

"How is that possible?" Halo stared at Raven; realisation hit him as he said, "you've been there before, without using anything?"

She stared at him, unmoving.

"Yes," she finally admitted.

"What is it? That place?"

"I don't know. Why do you think I know more than you?"

"Because you're in a place that you should not be able to access without some fucking device, that's why. We shouldn't be able to access it anyway. What the fuck is it? Some bizarre nightmare that some fucked up mind has invented and left for random people to fall into." He stared at her, "you don't have an implant, do you?"

"No."

"Would you know?"

"I think I would know," she said defensively.

Halo could feel the building up of tension in Raven by the way she held the sheet too tightly around her, and her bewilderment seemed to fill the air as though it were a tangible presence. Halo could feel it envelope him as he sat cold and sweating on the hard floor. It covered him like a sad ghost that won't believe that it is dead; it inched over him with its muddled tangled turmoil.

"What the fuck happened, Halo?"

"What?" It was his turn to feel confused.

"Well, I'm sitting here in your house half naked and its three a.m."

"You don't remember?"

"I remember meeting you. I remember us walking. I remember waking here and you telling me I had fainted. I remember the pizza, the champagne, the candles, and the music. I remember we danced. I felt dizzy. The night was so warm. It was like there was no air. It was hard to breathe. You were so close. You were kissing me. Your lips were on my neck, and I couldn't seem to breathe," she stopped and waited for Halo to say something.

"You fainted again."

"You kissed me? You took my dress off."

"And you kissed me and took my shirt off. You seemed to like what I was doing."

They stared at each other.

"Would you like me to drive you home?" he asked quietly.

"No," she said vehemently.

She pulled the sheet closer, a vague memory came to her, images of something dark and ominous walking through the water, and for a moment there was a flickering of something else, something even more threatening but it was too ephemeral to grasp.

"Is everything all right at home?" Halo asked. He knew how chaotic the place was she called home; a huge mansion where maybe a hundred people lived, some were family members, some transitory and passing through. It was a bohemian market that never, ever, closed. "When we were at the beach you asked to go somewhere safe? Why?"

She had moved back to the couch, she closed her eyes and lay back, wrapping herself up in the sheet even more. She looked very vulnerable. And yet when she had pulled him out of the slipstream she had been like some goddess, strong and immortal.

Halo stared at her, "I should thank you for pulling me out of that place. Because I'm not sure I could've made it out by myself." He said, "you were awesome."

She opened her eyes and looked at him.

"Seriously awesome," he repeated.

"I don't know how I got there. I really don't." She paused as she stared at him. "It was like I could feel that something was happening and then I was there; I could feel shapes pushing me forward, casually and gently, and they whispered in my ear, promises and delights. I was surrounded being moved away, which made me wonder what was happening, so I turned back." She took a deep breath, "you were so close, lying trussed up almost like an Egyptian mummy and you were spinning and falling, and I thought I have to bring him back because if I don't, that would be it."

"Thank you, I'm glad you did." He went over and squatted down in front of the couch and took one of her hands in his. He kissed the back of it. "It's late and we need to get some sleep. My sister is away; you can use her bedroom if you want somewhere more comfortable than the couch. Shall I take you there?"

"Thank you," she managed to give him a half smile.

Chapter Fourteen

Never forget: we walk on hell,
gazing at flowers.

Kobayashi Issa

The Past – Japan

"I know," Kimiko said on the night Namiyo broke off their engagement. "You have been called, the Gods have touched you, it's as plain to me as if they had drawn their signature across your forehead. You have a mission to complete."

"I will reimburse all the money your parents have put into the preparation for our wedding," he said quietly.

"I doubt there is much they have spent, considering we had not set a date. It will be fine," she replied.

"I should leave," he began.

"No," she replied. "You should stay, it's our last night. Let us share ourselves one more time. Tomorrow you can begin your new life."

The next day, Namiyo texted Tadahisa his banking details and the amount he was asking, "once the funds are in my account, you may come or send someone to pick up the sword. You will not be disappointed and there will be no discussion," he typed.

Namiyo was sitting at the desk giving the sword and its new handle a final polish, when the ping announced that the funds had been transferred. He packed the sword away, along with the remnants of the tusk. He had kept a small piece of ivory that he had carved into a stylised wave; he would wear this around his neck as a pendant for the rest of his life. It was his symbol of becoming the new Namiyo, a representation of his name – Wave – and that is what he would become, a wave that spread across the world.

He'd calculated that the money should last him at least seven years if he was frugal. He began packing up what he would need; some of his engraving tools, his computer, some books, clothes; everything would easily fit in his car. He had booked a room in a house on Nagashima Island for a month with the option to extend. His mother was devastated and wrongly assuming he was heartbroken – he assured her he was fine. He stood outside his studio amid the peaceful bamboos and said goodbye, knowing he would never return. He would miss this place and he would miss Mizuki, who he decided would be happier here.

Mizuki had other plans; she had found a cosy spot within his bags on the back seat and was travelling with him. He didn't realise until he was halfway to his destination when he saw her in the mirror, standing up and doing a long stretch before turning around and settling back down again.

***

Kimiko also joined him, six months later.

"Your first disciple," she announced when she arrived at his small apartment at Reihoku. And so began their life together as brother and sister, master and disciple, although as the months and years progressed, she took over the entire running of the organisation.

She was fluent in five languages and taught him enough English and French so he could record his videos in three languages. She provided the subtitles for some other languages and found others that would do the work she couldn't. Slowly people began to join them, first five, then twenty. When they reached fifty, Kimiko found an old hotel near Nagasaki and really got to work. She set up a publishing company and a website, published two of his books; one in Japanese and another in English, and began the translations in another six languages. By now there were two hundred people that had joined, and a waiting list for another five hundred. She bought a resort style complex on Oshiba Island that had fallen on hard times and could accommodate most of them, as well as be used for week-long seminars. They had moved from small halls to large conference centres. She organised a hierarchy of workers and ran the whole organisation with a silky smooth smile on her tranquil face that hid a core of steel.

This left Namiyo to concentrate on communicating his visions and beliefs, and how best to bring the earth back from the brink of destruction.

Nami no Michi – 波の道 – The Way of the Wave was what they were called. As more of his visions manifested in the world, the more his prophecies resonated with people everywhere.

They were invited to attend conferences in the United States and throughout South America and Europe. Through a mistranslation they attended the Great Tribulation and

Rapture summit in California, and from then on they became known as part of the Pacific Rim Rapturists. Namiyo thought it was hilarious, but Kimiko was more troubled, knowing that being labelled as a doomsday cult would create its own problems. But it did bring more followers than either anticipated. Within five years the organisation had centres in ten different countries. They bought an island in the Seto inland sea, using the resort on Oshiba Island, which had grown extensively since the original purchase and now had a private jetty, a perfect launching site to their island that was only ten minutes away, and there a serene sanctuary was built for the inner sanctum of the group.

***

Maeve went every night; she couldn't say why she did and she couldn't understand half of what she heard, but the sheer cadence and rhythm of the way he spoke produced in her a peacefulness that was so soothing and wonderful, that she had to keep coming back. On the fifth and final night she was presented with a beautiful gilt-edged envelope by one of the attendants, and inside was an invitation to dinner with Kimiko and Namiyo. She smiled all the way through the talk.

One of the attendants came and led her to a small room near the front entrance of the auditorium. She brushed her hair, thinking that maybe she should have put some make-up on, wondering why she had been singled out. But she wasn't nervous – she was excited, and the usual intense anxiety that normally accompanied her daily, had receded. An elegant woman came in and introduced herself as Kimiko, although Maeve already knew her from the program and booklets she'd been reading. She sat beside her and explained that the two of them would leave soon for the restaurant and they would meet Namiyo there.

"He is intrigued that you came to every lecture, some come to two, but he thinks you may be the first one who chose to attend all lectures in their city. Please, there is no need to feel you need to offer a reason why. He thinks that maybe you have questions that he can answer or maybe there is something else he can offer you; some insight into your own personal life." She paused for a moment, "he has many healing gifts, so please know that his intention to help is quite genuine."

The first thing Maeve noticed about him was that he was much slenderer than he appeared on stage and much quieter. There was an aura of stillness around him, that she had never seen before on anyone, it was as though he inhabited a different space to what they inhabited. He was very soft spoken as well, which surprised her, as on stage his voice seemed to fill the whole of the auditorium.

He was intrigued by her name and asked her where it was from.

"It's Irish," she said, adding with a slight blush, "it means, she who intoxicates, also there is a very famous Irish warrior queen of that name, known as a fair-haired wolf queen, who was so beautiful, that one glance could rob a man of two-thirds of his courage."

He laughed uproariously at that, "intoxicate, what a wonderful word," he said. "As you can see, English is a language I'm still striving to understand fully. How would you describe its meaning?"

"Well, it usually means to get someone drunk, but I guess it also means to be excited or enthralled by something," she replied, laughing before adding, "I'm not anything like my name."

"Allow me to disagree with you," he said. "I think you are more that equal to the meaning. My name means wave-man, hence I wear this pendant to always remind me of the moment I chose to embody my name. To become more than I had been before, to become more than I thought was possible. These last eight years," he glanced at Kimiko, "is that correct? Eight years?"

She nodded.

"These eight years have certainly been nothing like I had expected, I was merely hoping I would not be considered some mad, crazy man ranting away to nobody. Maybe I am a mad crazy man, but people want to hear me. What I say makes sense to them. Maybe they are all mad and crazy too."

"Maybe it's because the world is so mad and crazy and what you offer makes us feel safer somehow," she said very quietly, staring into his dark eyes.

"I hope that what I offer, can somehow make a differ-ence, because I don't see our beautiful earth becoming less dramatic, quite the opposite," he replied soberly. "But, I also think each one of us must become all that we can be so we can tip the balance, and give the children being born a future."

"Do you have children?" she asked.

"No," he replied. "Do you?"

"I have a son," she replied. "It's so hard with everything that is happening. Each summer we either have huge bush fires that ring our city, turning the air so smoky, it's hard to breathe. Or it rains so much there is flooding or the storms that build along the coast and create huge waves that batter our coastline causing a different type of flooding. In the last month there have been earthquakes, three quite big ones, there have never been earthquakes here," she looked at the two across from her. "I'm sorry that must sound so pathetic to you, you deal with earthquakes almost weekly."

"Yes, that is true," Kimiko answered. "But our whole country has worked out ways to help us feel safer and yet we are all still apprehensive whenever the earth begins to move."

Maeve looked away, wondering if she should stop before she said something so terrible, they would wish they hadn't invited her.

"I wonder why I brought my son into the world, did I have that right? What have I passed on to him? I only discovered a few years ago that my grandfather, who died before I was born, had been conscripted to the Vietnam war. He came home very unwell, and some of the toxins, these terrible poisons that were used, not only affected his health but also affected his DNA and were passed down to his children and grandchildren. I've been lucky I don't at this point have anything, but my son Connor had quite bad health issues when he was born. He seems strong now, but I don't know," she paused seeing Connor sleeping, her child, his strange ugly face a reminder of what else might be lurking inside him, at any moment manifesting into some of the terrible diseases that her elder brother was dealing with and what his young daughter had recently died from.

"Sometimes I think I don't love him as I should, that I withhold my love because I can't bare it. I don't want to feel what I'll feel if he dies from something I've given him. Or because our world has become so toxic, or another terrible virus mutates, and this times it will be the children who are vulnerable to it. You must think I'm terrible saying all of that," she looked down at her hands, willing herself not to cry.

She saw his hand reach over and cover her hands., "I think you are very honest and there is courage in saying out loud what you feel. Do you talk to your husband about this?"

Maeve shook her head, "he's dealing with his own problems. He's a fire fighter and is exhausted half the time. He's very different from me; he thinks I'm too sensitive."

"We all have to be what we are. Your sensitivity is also your strength if you accept it and embody it," his hand was still over hers. "Perhaps I should tell you how you appeared to me when I saw you sitting there the first night, and then the second, and then the next. It was your flaming red hair that made me first notice you; it was such a radiant colour, so very beautiful, and it made me think of Amaterasu. She is the Sun Goddess of Japan. Her full name Amaterasu Omikami means 'goddess of the most high who shines on the world.' She is the eldest of the three divine children and she was given divine right to rule. This is one of her stories.

"The youngest of the three, the impetuous storm god Susanoo, resented his elder sister and began to misbehave badly. He ruined the rice crop, defecated in the sacred temple and rampaged through her domain. He killed her animals, threw her pony at her loom killing one of her favourite assistants, a weaver. Amaterasu felt responsible for what her brother had done, as she had been too soft on him and kept excusing his wild behaviour. She was so overcome with guilt and remorse that she went into hiding; she went into a cave and using her magic, sealed the entrance with the Heavenly Rock. With the Sun gone, Heaven and Earth were plunged into darkness and chaos.

"After almost a year, the Kami, the Gods, gathered for an emergency meeting to work out a way to coerce Amaterasu out of hiding. They decided to lure her out with curiosity –

so, all the cockerels, vassals of the Sun Goddess, were asked to crow altogether at once. Then, the one-eyed smith was asked to rhythmically hit an iron nail into a hard rock. Together they created music. Ishikoridome, God of mirror makers, was instructed to make a large mirror, and Tamano'oya, God of jewellery makers, to make a string of jade beads as long as the mirror. Ameno-uzume, Goddess of the Dawn and the Arts, adorned her body with ferns and flowers and began to dance on top of an upside down wooden tub. She stomped on the tub making even more noise, soon all the Gods joined in the dance, laughing and cheering. Hearing all the noise, Amaterasu slid the rock to look out at what was going on, there she could see the mirror, and fascinated by the light, Amaterasu came out of the cave. The Gods threw a *shimenawa,* a sacred rope over the entrance to prevent her running back. Amaterasu's light re-entered the world, illuminating the chaos. Ashamed, she begged forgiveness for her actions, but the Gods gathered around her, bowing deeply, they praised her greatness more than ever before." His eyes were still gazing into hers, the most compassionate eyes she had ever looked into.

"Maeve," Namiyo said softly, "it's very important to discern what one is responsible for, and for what one is not in any way responsible for. Because guilt and regret for what we have no control over will dim and shadow our radiance, the effect of that spills over into everything and everyone. You cannot hold yourself responsible for what was done to your grandfather and the repercussions of that, or for what is happening to the world. I understand why you feel like you do, but your radiance must shine like the sun; its important. We are all important. Love is so important, it is by far, the most important gift we possess and which we can share endlessly."

"Thank you," she whispered. He squeezed her hand.

"Here comes the food. Food is also very important," he said with a laugh.

It was during the meal, she decided she would like to go to Japan and attend some of the meditations and work-shops that she had read were on offer. Surely, she would be able to go for a month, there was money she had saved up from her part-time job, and she would learn practices that would help her cope better so she could be with her son, and despite her fears – become the mother she had always wanted to be, the one she felt she had so failed at being. The thought made her so happy that she found herself laughing more than she had for years, and feeling so grateful that fate had somehow bought Kimiko and Namiyo to her, and knowing that she was somehow linked to them and somehow important to them as well.

She didn't realise that her decision would change every-thing. That her three-week stay in Japan would turn into years as a new virulent and deadly pandemic would circle the globe quarantining all the countries. Or that her husband would refuse her any contact with her son, and that despite everything she tried, she would not ever see him again.

Chapter Fifteen

Delusion is not being aware of your Fundamental mind.
Enlightenment is realizing your Fundamental Essence.

Mazu

The intercom buzzed late one night; Halo looked at the two people standing there, a man with an incredibly ugly face and a very tall woman, with short silver-blonde hair. He had no idea who they were until the man flashed his badge and announced his name. Halo buzzed them up and wondered if he had inadvertently strayed into some secure no-go zone. The slipstream, was it military? He opened the door.

"What have I done now?" he asked in a humorous tone.

The man smiled and said, "I don't know. What have you done? Do you have a guilty conscience?" he paused and smiled at Halo, surprisingly it lessened the unsightliness of his features. "I am aware of your past transgressions, but we're not here because of those or any new ones you may have committed. We have come to you to see if you might help us trace someone."

"Perhaps we should sit," the man added.

Halo pulled a chair and sat down at the dining table and the other two sat across from him. The tall woman was very striking; she hadn't shown her badge, Halo recalled, so he turned and spoke to the man first. "Superintendent Inspector have I got that right?"

"Yes, you can call me Connor if you like," the man said. He might be ugly, but there was something warm and approachable about him, Halo decided. Connor pushed over his pad. A photo of a teenager appeared changing from sepia to a more modern palate. "I believe you know this young lady."

Halo looked at the photo — Raven stared up at him.

"She's not in trouble, but we are quite concerned about her. Do you know where she might be? We have tried her registered address, but they say she has moved."

That surprised Halo, he had spoken to her only a few nights ago and she had not mentioned moving then.

"We need to talk to her, if you can contact her would you ask her to call me?" Connor passed over his wafer and said, "we don't need to know where she is, but we would like to know that she is there of her free will."

"Do you think she has been abducted?"

Jo and Connor exchanged glances.

"Halo," Connor said, "can I trust you with this? It's important. Your name came up in a search we did on her. I understand that the two of you may occasionally commit the odd transgression online. I'm not interested in your hacking or even what she may or may not have been involved in, understand? She is someone that we have been searching for, ever since she was born. A man was found dead, a strand of hair was taken from his hands, and the DNA was linked to her." Connor paused; he could hardly believe that his old friend over at forensics had contacted him with the information, linking this DNA to the dead woman, his sister. And even more surprising, since Carnies rarely went to hospitals preferring their own doctors, yet Raven had been taken to a local hospital after a childhood fall, and after some tests her DNA had been recorded. The Carnies must've considered her extremely important for them to take her there.

"Halo, we think this man may have attacked Raven. It was over in the old Quarantine zone, is that somewhere she goes? Do you know? Has she ever mentioned going there?"

"The Ghostlands? Is that what you're referring to?" Halo asked. "Yeah, she sometimes goes there but she hasn't said anything about being attacked."

"We aren't after her because of this. The dead man was well known to us, a registered sex offender, only just released from prison. As I said, she is of interest to us because of the circumstances of her birth."

"She doesn't know her birth parents," Halo said quietly.

"We can talk to her about that," Connor said gently. "There is also a rather large inheritance, which is hers as long as we can verify her legitimacy, which is fairly certain judging by the DNA result."

Halo looked over at the woman. There was something familiar about her. "Do I know you?" he asked.

She laughed. "We have met online, I occasionally make forays into the shadowy nexus."

"You're not a cop?"

"Well spotted."

She had the most amazing eyes, he thought, almost a translucent aqua.

"So, Halo, you'll let her know it's urgent she contacts us. I promise I won't be putting a stinger on her. I just want to talk." Connor said.

"I'll try to contact her," Halo replied.

"I appreciate it," Connor said. He and the woman stood up. "Any help you can give us."

***

Halo sat and thought about what to do. He finally sent her a message requesting a chat at one of the secure booths. They promised five minutes of absolute privacy, safe from government surveillance and outlaw on-sellers. Halo knew it was more likely that they would have three minutes before the security would be breached, but it was the best he could think of.

It took two messages to get a reply and then they plunged in, connecting into a hundred or so random interlocks until they sat across from each other in a cosy, velvet-lined virtual booth. Her avatar, a black winged moth, sat across from his, a spinning figure eight symbol of black light. He told her about his two visitors; she didn't seem surprised. He asked her where she was, and he could sense her hesitation. They were already into one minute, so he pushed the question again.

"Yes," she answered. "I am somewhere different. Two women came for me and took me to this penthouse, I don't know where. Out of the zone. It has something to do with my parents." Halo felt his sense of dread grow, this seemed wrong somehow. Time was ticking though. They were now three and a half minutes down.

"Will you call the cop?" he asked.

"I don't know," she said.

"Can we meet?"

She hesitated before saying, "I'll let you know."

There were undulations in the velvet walls; the first warning that systems were being breached.

Fuck, Halo thought, *I've never seen that happen so fast.*

They both pulled out simultaneously.

***

Raven stood up and walked away from the screen. The room was permanently at the most comfortable temperature, but she found herself feeling chilled. She looked out of the floor-to-ceiling windows, an impossibly huge night sky filled up her vision. Beneath it a black sea churned, a maelstrom of white foam crested water. Her apartment was at the very top of the building; it was opulent and like something that movie stars lived in. She wished she were back in her tiny room, shabby it may have been, but at least she felt safe there. There didn't seem any way to escape; she could certainly move around within this luxurious place but she doubted they would let her leave. It was a prison, albeit one that wanted to please her.

When the two women had first shown up two days ago, Aurora had been in tears even as she brusquely told Raven to pack. Raven's first thought was that she had been sold. It had happened to others she knew. She had realised when she was still quite young that she was more a possession of the Carnie's – there for them to use as they wished. That her skills and natural attributes worked so well with their online activities meant she was an asset, and was unlikely to be directed to earn her keep somewhere else like the entertainment districts that they ran.

She had left in the long black limousine, a relic from another era. It moved so silently and with the black tinted windows she couldn't even see where she was going. The women had spoken softly, assuring her that she was finally coming home, that she had been missing for a very long time; since she had been born, in fact. They told her that her father, someone called Sebastian van Elson – and their voices took on a reverential tone as they said his name – was a very famous and brilliant scientist, and they were taking her to his estate; the headquarters of his institute.

Will he be there? She had asked. Unfortunately, he had died before she had been born, they said. What about my mother, she had asked. They had both shaken their heads; no, sadly she was also dead.

And now a policeman was looking for her as well. She felt like her world had turned upside down. She felt more alone than she thought was possible as she stared at the dark angry sea that was tossing itself against the sandstone cliffs and wondered about Ceriful. He seemed to have disappeared and her brain was clearer too; the endless buzzing had lessened to the point that it was like a low-level white noise hum. The place must have a buffer, she thought or maybe it's because it was so far out of the city.

She sat down on the one of the big comfy chairs, which moulded seamlessly into her shape and tried to relax. She had everything she had ever wanted. It was all here. She had craved solitude and peace, and now she was surrounded by it. Luxury enclosed her, and she was able to buy anything she wanted, or so the women had implied. The women had names, but she refused to think of them; she didn't want to like them or think of them as friends. They were strangers, and she figured that they were being paid to do this.

Friends, did she actually have any? Aurora cared about her, but her influence was limited; she was Raven's caregiver, she had been brought in when it became obvious that Raven had a very lucrative skill, and she was there to make sure that

Raven was physically well and available, the fact that she was so kind-natured was a blessing. The other Carnies were just that – people she knew, some were brusque but ok, some were sleazy and creepy, some she knew reasonably well, but weren't friends, even calling them acquaintances seemed like a stretch.

Halo, she realised was her only friend. She sat very still for a long moment and thought about that. It was true, she had no doubt, and theirs had almost been an instantaneous bond, almost as though they had always known each other.

***

She closed her eyes and felt herself slipping, just like that; seamlessly and effortlessly she dropped into the slipstream. As she floated there, she realised that it was different this time – turbulent and unsettled. She could feel the agitation and something else – anger she thought – is that what she could feel? She felt buffeted by it; pulled around as if in an invisible rip. This time the slipstream was devoid of light, black on black with flashes of deep red and an even deeper indigo. There was an electric pulse going through her as well. It was almost painful. Even as she thought that, the pain intensified. What was happening? She tried to pull out, break away, and leave. She didn't seem able to.

Suddenly Halo's words came into her head, something he had said; 'do you ever wonder about slipping out? Well, about not slipping out?'

The current was pulling her along more fiercely. She tried to make herself slow down, but that only made her go faster. She panicked.

I'm not going to make it out, she thought.

She remembered Halo and how she had pulled him out, and how hard that had been. Her vision was blurring she was moving so fast.

No, she thought. *I'm not staying here.* She screamed; "LET ME GO! NOW!"

Her chair flew backwards and she landed on the floor. The large screen exploded, glass shards flew past her, one tiny sliver embedded in her cheek. The lights exploded, the small down lights in the ceiling, as well as the large fancy globe shaped lamps near the window. All exploded simultaneously, then the enormous movie screen on the wall imploded a few seconds later. Suddenly, the two women were in the room along with a security guard. They helped her up. The room was dark, but outside the night sky was alive with what seemed like a dozen lightning flashes. As she looked out at the sea that had become even wilder, she saw what seemed like an enormous sea monster with massive tentacles rise from the waves and let loose a roar.

She could feel the glass beneath her bare feet cutting into the skin of her soles, she cried out and the security guard picked her up and carried her into the bathroom. The two women cleaned her feet, and carefully pulled out the glass speck in her cheek. One of them insisted on running a bath, complete with a small glass of cognac beside the candles they had also insisted on lighting. She lay in the warm water; her heart thumping too fast and too erratic, submerged to her neck while the rose and lavender bubbles scented the air, and she thought back to the slipstream.

All she could think was that something had made it angry, but anger is an emotion she thought. How could it feel? How could it have feelings? What the hell is it?

Chapter Sixteen

*"Summer night: even the stars
are whispering to each other."*

Kobayashi Issa

The Past – Japan

"You know he is in love with you?" Kimiko said bluntly. "As you are with him."

Maeve looked at the woman beside her, whom she had come to think of as a sister; they were both sitting under one of the large black pine trees that were probably a few hundred years old and cast wonderful shade on these hot summer afternoons. Mizuki was laying on her lap, stretched out and elongated as far as it was possible, so the cooler sea breeze ruffled her fur, this tree being one of her favourite resting spots.

"You know it is true. And you need to do something about it." Kimiko continued, "he will not make the first move. Namiyo would feel it inappropriate and would wonder if you were only going along with it because of what he is, not because you have feelings for him. Or that maybe you are still heartbroken, and the timing is wrong. I know you still grieve for your son, but the future will unfold however it will, meanwhile there is this moment. This present time."

"I can't believe his ex-fiancé is trying to match make us." Maeve replied with a smile.

Kimiko laughed. "Someone has to. You know he and I fell in together; of course, we had feelings for each other. I love him more than anyone else I know. I don't think either of us was in love with each other in the way you both are, though. We came from the same class, we were well suited, he was so different from the other men though, so poetic, creative and spiritual, and that appealed to me immensely. I think our marriage would've worked well." She paused and laughed. "We basically have that marriage now, with me organising everything and allowing him space to do his work. I have reached my potential in a way I could never have done in a normal marriage. And I love it. I know my skills provide the framework for his message to go out and be heard. I'm immensely happy. And, I have my discreet dalliances and that works very well for me." She grinned.

"Has he actually said that he is in love with me?"

"No, of course not. He is very private, but he talks about you endlessly; he will mention something you said to him, or something that you observed and pointed out, or picked up, like a shell or driftwood that you bring back from one of your walks together. He will smile, and the love he feels will just beam out of his face as he says your name – he says it as if it is a special mantra that holds everything, and then he will repeat the story again, just so he can relive that moment, and smile again."

"Do you think it's going to rain? There are so many clouds on the horizon," Maeve asked, as she stared out across the still waters of the sea that encircled the island.

"Don't change the subject. It's not going to rain tonight, it's going to be a clear full moon night and the two of you are going to go for a romantic walk along the beach. And you are going to tell him how you feel."

"But what if…?"

"There is no what if anything. I suspect he fell in love with you the moment he saw you. What was the word? Intoxicated. Yes, you intoxicated him, and he is still intoxicated. Maeve, the two of you will make each other so happy. You already do. If any two people in the world deserve that, it's the two of you," Kimiko said with finality in her voice that Maeve knew was irrefutable.

***

"What shall we name this child, our beautiful treasure?" Namiyo asked, as he held their tiny daughter.

Maeve smiled despite her exhaustion. The birth had been relatively easy, but the earthquake that had rocked their island and come as her baby had entered the world had made many of her fears and anxieties rise to the surface. She sipped the green tea with fresh lemon pieces and lotus-flower petals that Kimiko had brought in for her. It was her favourite tea and it soothed her — somewhat.

"She is a treasure; something very precious," Maeve agreed.

"What about Junko Takara? Junko is pure child and Takara is treasure, something very precious." Namiyo said.

"Yes, let's call her that," Maeve agreed.

"Her hair is so black, do you think it will change and become autumn-hued like yours?"

"No, I think she will have black hair, my dear," Maeve said with a smile.

"Perhaps our next daughter will have your flame hair." He replied as he stared down at his daughter and gently stroked her thick, black locks.

Then Maeve noticed it – it would have been indiscernible to anyone else, the way his eyes momentarily became unfocused, and a certain something shifted invisibly around him, and then he was as before.

"What did you see?" Maeve asked, feeling uneasy.

"What?" Namiyo blinked. "Nothing really; nothing to do with anything. I saw three foxes sitting together."

"Kitsune?"

"Maybe. Three is a very lucky number, so three Kitsune can only be a blessing," he replied softly.

Chapter Seventeen

Death, tho I see him not, is near.

Walter Savage Landor

"**C**an I invite someone to visit me?" Raven asked Woman A.

Woman A said, "maybe."

"Or should I go out and meet him out there?" she asked.

"That can be arranged."

"Then I'd like to do that. Tomorrow."

Woman A walked over and conferred with Woman B.

Woman B came over and said, "we can arrange for an afternoon out. Perhaps you would like to meet your friend for lunch."

It surprised her how glad she was to see Halo when she walked into the small but very exclusive café. The café was in a part of the city she had not been before. There were still shops here, boutiques mainly; selling exquisite outfits with prices that had almost made her stop breathing. The women had insisted she enter one, and try some shoes on and she ended up with some black leather boots that were so soft, they felt like skin and another pair of red sparkly heels.

"Been shopping?" he asked as she set down the two huge bags.

"Shoes," she said wryly. "I had to please my two minders. They were very insistent."

"So, your new life is going well?" he asked.

"A luxurious cage is still a cage."

"Is that what it is?"

"It feels that way," Raven said as she looked at the gardens that surrounded the complex; the grass seemed so green, the flowers so vibrantly bright. There were tiny-jewelled birds that hovered around the blooms, alighting for a moment then flying off in a blur of iridescent wings. She wondered if there was anything real out there. It looked too perfect.

He picked up the menu, looking at the prices, "you're paying aren't you?"

"I guess."

They ordered starters and then a shared platter of seafood. Halo asked if she had thought about contacting the detective.

She shook her head. "Not yet. I'm not sure if I will."

Halo sensed she had a Carnie's mistrust of authority.

"He may have some answers," he persisted. He wondered why he was pushing this but there was something about the man's sincerity that had impressed him.

"They have given me a file on my father, Sebastian van Elson, its huge with reports and interviews, and films of him speaking at conferences and videos of him addressing the media. He was an impressive man, a geneticist and climatologist; a genius it seems, he was very eloquent and charismatic, his organisation continues following his manifesto," she stopped. It had been a bit overwhelming reading and watching all that was on offer.

"What about your mother?" Halo asked.

"There is some information about her. Takara is her name, she grew up in Japan; her father was an artist and head of a strange religious cult. Her upbringing was eccentric, and very different from my father's." Raven remembered the few photographs of her; she thought she could see a resemblance there, in the delicate petite features they both shared. "She was a Remote Viewer. Do you know what that is?"

Halo shook his head.

"She could see events and people that were in a different location or different countries; sometimes they were in the present and sometimes in the future. She saw them inside her mind. She could hear them talking. That's how she met him. She contacted him after seeing some disturbing images that related to a conference he was about to attend."

Raven thought about the small private wedding, she had watched the film of that at least twenty times. Her mother had looked happy she'd thought. But, reading between the lines of what she'd been given, she felt their marriage had caused friction within his organisation. One of the men who had not been invited to the wedding had been her father's best friend, Mars Lodstrom.

There had been quite a bit of coverage of Sebastian's death – his ship and all onboard had gone missing in a huge storm off the coast of South America, and even though the wreckage had never been found, there had been no doubt that all had perished. There had been a photo of her mother, dressed in a black kimono, at least five months pregnant at the memorial service. There was no information on how she had died and how Raven had ended up where she had, which struck her as rather odd.

"Do you know what happened to them?"

"Him, yes. But not her, and not how I ended up with the Carnies."

"The detective said you went missing after you were born," Halo said. "He may have some more information."

"I'll think about talking to him."

The first course of their meal turned up, so they concentrated on trying out the six small tapas dishes, and Halo steered the conversation onto more general topics as they ate.

He poured her a small glass from the jug of fruity sangria that had arrived.

"Have you been back in?" he asked. "The slipstream?"

She hesitated, "a few nights ago," she admitted. "It was scary. There was anger and rage, and I really didn't think I would be able to get out. I did, but…"

Halo waited. She told him about what had happened when she pulled out.

"They," she gestured over at the two women who were having their dinner at a nearby table, "say it was a massive power surge caused by the huge lightning storm that was raging outside at the time, but I know that's not true. That's not what it was."

"Raven, I've been thinking about this, the slipstream as we call it, what it might be. I've searched around, and to be quite honest even though there is some wacky stuff out there, there is nothing that even faintly sounds like what we have experienced." He paused for a moment, trying to pull all the divergent threads of his thoughts into something coherent and clear so he could actually put them into words. "There is something I keep coming back to." He stared out the window for a moment. "Our world is now so fused with this unreal – yet hyperreal – online world that we can barely function without it. The AI that is part of everything online is elusive, and hard to get a handle on. At times, it feels clunky and ridiculous, yet how much do we really understand of how everything works? Even you and I – we recognise the coding and cryptography that swims below the surface – yet I know I come across random keys and signs that look like secret messages. When people talk about this, they always just call it garbage code, flotsam that the Internet regurgitates into the corners; old stuff that's now irrelevant.

"People wonder who controls it all and many times it's the IT Corps that people look at or governments, but they all only control a small fraction of it. They say no one does. So, what does that mean? That the world web has somehow organically become its own self-functioning entity, and if you continue with that thought and some have, then is there a consciousness that sits in the middle of this web and is, if not controlling, then influencing us, directly or subtly? And what is this entity? Benign? Dictatorial? Malignant? And does it have full consciousness?"

He paused and looked at Raven. "Because this entity – for want of a better word – has access to everything that has ever been written, filmed, sung, or made into art. To our mythologies, our histories, our politic rhetoric, our religions, our science. To our news, fake or real. To everything that we have discussed, discovered, or analysed. To our thoughts, our dreams, all those stupid narcissist rambles that people continue to broadcast. To our fears, our nightmares, or the dark and psychotic deeds we have done, or thought of doing."

He poured himself a drink, "so, maybe this slipstream is part of the web's consciousness, or maybe it's subconscious. And I feel – and it's an instinctual feeling – that I'm not far from the truth."

"It sort of makes sense. Did we fall in, or were we invited? Why would it want us in there?" Raven asked.

"Perhaps it wanted to study us on a more personal level. Perhaps it needs something we have." As he spoke, he noticed she had gone very pale. "Raven, are you all right?" Halo asked.

"Maybe the reason I can connect into it has something to do with my mother; she was a remote viewer, and maybe I have that skill too. Maybe that is how I can be there without a device, because I do; I can just flow into it." She stared at him, her voice shaking.

"It's slipping out," she said. "Whatever is in the slipstream, some of it is seeping into our world. I see things. Creatures; nightmare creatures – I have for some time. I see them here in our world, but no one else does, or they don't react, so I'm presuming they're not seeing them."

She stopped as the plates were cleared from the table. She looked out the window. Small fairy like creatures had landed on some large orange hibiscus flowers. They fluttered there with their transparent wings and the long scorpion like stings that protruded from their backs. They were watching her, and their pretty faces smiled at her – but not in a friendly way. In the air behind them, their stingers flashed bronze and silver in the sunlight.

"Can you see some now?" he asked.

She nodded. "It was angry the other night. Disturbed – but by what? Something we'd done? Something I had done?" she asked.

"Perhaps it was you saving me. Perhaps it didn't want you to. Perhaps it wanted me out of the way," Halo said softly.

He thought back to his dream; the images as strong as a memory, the stranger warning him to keep away. Why was he a threat? Why did it need Raven? Were those two things even connected to the slipstream?

Their main dish had arrived, and Raven was looking at it in horror.

"What are you seeing?" he asked.

A mass of writhing limbs; dismembered legs and arms, torsos ripped open, their innards spilling out, and brains pulsing out of skulls that had been exposed. Everything was rippling and moving, as though it were alive. She closed her eyes, fighting down the nausea.

She shook her head. "I'd rather not say."

"I can't eat it," she pushed it closer to Halo.

He looked at it, the usual morsels that lie on a Seafood platter; prawns, crab, mussels, oysters and calamari. Her face was so filled with revulsion that he decided he was unlikely to enjoy it. He called the waiter over and asked if they would take the platter over to the two women.

"Is something wrong?" the man asked.

"We're both quite full after the starters," he said, smiling. "Perhaps we can have some coffee."

He took her hand in his and said, "we'll work it out, you know."

"Maybe. Even if we begin to understand it, what can we do? Realistically, what could we possibly do against whatever this is?"

"I don't know, but there's always something."

The coffee arrived and she asked if they could take it and have it on the verandah. She looked at the fairies with their faces pressed against the glass. She wasn't going to let them stop her. The waiter directed them to a couch with plump green and blue cushions under the verandah where honey-suckle grew rampantly. They sat together and sipped their coffee. Raven was relieved to see that the fairies had flown off.

Halo moved a fraction closer until they were sitting side by side. Her eyes were so large and grey, as though she had her own private storm gathering there. He moved his face towards her, so their cheeks were touching and then their mouths met, and Raven responded with a kiss that was sweet and fragile and too brief. She moved away. She felt giddy, unsteady, as though his touch produced in her a volatile substance that took over her body, her skin, her bones.

She glanced up at the sky, a mass of clouds ominously full and brooding, had gathered in the sky, the billowing darkness moving furiously, covering the sun in seconds. A lightning flash lit up the garden; lit up Halo's face and her face in a split second of brightness. The thunder that rolled over them was less intense, but just as ear shattering. Halo kissed Raven again. He could feel her heart beating, could taste the coffee on her lips, her breath on his cheek, her eyelashes fluttering against his face like the wings of a butterfly. Another kiss, this one more intense, and the storm moved around them; the lightning flashed in the clouds and the thunder answered as though it was responding to a song that only it could hear. Finally, she pushed him away.

Halo tipped his head back and stared at the black mass of clouds that were churning and boiling like an overflowing cauldron.

When he spoke, his voice was very low, so she struggled to hear, "I used to wonder what it was like to be in love. I didn't really believe there was such a thing. I thought it was just made up; like a clever marketing ploy to sell songs, sell movies. I understood love as something like caring for your parents and friends. I understood desire, lust, wanting someone so badly that it hurt. But I didn't understand being in love. I had never felt it."

He looked at her. "I think about you way too much. I don't actually like this feeling. It's like I'm out of control, even drugs have not ever been this wild, this unstable. I would prefer not to feel this way, but I do."

"It's not love," she said firmly, although her heart was beating so loud it seemed to fill up the space between them, like the thunder that was rumbling above.

"Then what is it? And why don't you think it is love?"

"Because love is not like that," she said.

"Not like that. Then what is it like? Love is gentle. Love is kind. Love is romantic," he said the phrases in a sardonic litany. "Bullshit; love is primeval. Love came crawling with us when we pulled ourselves out of the swamp ten million years ago. Love is savage. Love is all consuming, devouring like some beast. Love is hunger."

Raven felt herself being pulled in two directions; the past where everything between them was just a game – just a laugh – and the future that swirled with intensity and passions that she didn't want to admit to. "I can't deal with this. Everything is changing. My whole life is different. It's all too fast," Raven blurted out. "But, I do feel for you."

A wind came out of nowhere and buffeted them, the air crackled around them.

"But what do you feel?" Halo asked.

"I don't know," Raven said softly, like the falling of a leaf; almost indiscernible.

She stared at him. It was at that moment that the clouds decided to let loose the water that had filled them to bursting point. The rain poured down, warm and torrential, soaking them and everything, within minutes.

Chapter Eighteen

*When the stars threw down their spears, and watered heaven with
their tears,
Did he smile his work to see?
Did he who made the lamb make thee?*

William Blake

Raven walked through the empty halls of the art gallery. She began to hurry until she was almost running. She felt distraught. She was looking for something. It was important. She must find it. She had so little time. The paintings hung silently on the wall as though they mocked her, as though they knew what she was looking for, but had decided to reveal nothing. She was becoming breathless, and the halls were unending. She stopped, on the floor she noticed that flower petals lay in untidy heaps. She looked up at the painting, it contained a figure like an angel; he was standing on top of a great jagged mountain and the sky was covered in clouds of silver and gold. The figure turned and reached out his hand. His arm came out of the frame, out of the picture and she instinctively put out her hand to receive his. She felt his fingers lock around hers and then he pulled her in, her feet left the ground and she entered the picture.

Raven stood on the mountain; the rocks were hard and uneven, and all around was the majestic canopy of the heavens with their shafts of golden light spilling over her. Faraway in the distance she could see the gallery, as though she was looking at it through a tiny window, so very distant and removed. She looked at the figure next to her. He was tall and had wings of such cold whiteness that they seemed to have been carved from ice. He was all in white; his body encased in material that was as shiny as a pearl. His face was pale, and his hair was as white a blonde as she had ever seen. When he spoke, it was like listening to the wind.

"This is your world," he said as he gestured to all that lay beneath them.

Raven looked down, how small and peculiar it was, she felt strangely detached like the world at her feet meant nothing to her. She looked at the angel, was he an angel? What else could he be with those wings? His eyes were amethyst crystals. His face was more beautiful than any angel that had ever been painted in all the centuries past. It was terrifyingly exquisite.

"Or, if you prefer, here is my world," the angel said.

The wind whistled the words around in an icy rapture. Raven looked down into the abyss again; cities of cold crystal sprung up from the snow-covered valleys; cities carved from glass and ice. Rainbow lights shone from their fractured sides and lit up the snow so it became a fairytale world of wondrous hues, covered in glittering stardust. Away from the cities, thick forests of pine and conifer grew, interrupted only by the glacial lakes that shone like mirrors in the noonday sun. It was a cold world and she could feel the numbing chill, but it made up for its arctic breath with a shining clarity of light; the green foliage of the pines was like velvet, and the rainbow lights were so fragile yet so striking, like chimes made into colour. They struck the snow and exploded into colour upon colour. And there was music – a haunting siren's call that called to her, sublime and wonderful.

"Which world do you choose?" the angel asked beguilingly.

Raven looked into his face again. His face so very beautiful that she could hardly breathe. How could she answer? Why was she being asked? She didn't understand.

"Are the choices so difficult?" his voice floated over her like gentle snowflakes.

The angel laughed, and his mirth trickled over her like a joyful waterfall.

The angel covered her with his wings, his hands that clasped her to him, were cold yet fiery. She could feel his body against hers, could feel his breath. She did not want to look up and into that face of awesome beauty.

"You must choose," his voice whispered into her ear.

He lifted her off the ground and the two of them were falling, descending silently and slowly, falling like snowflakes do. His wings of ice enclosed their two bodies as they dropped.

Why doesn't he open his wings? she thought. *Why doesn't he use them to fly? Why must we fall?* But the descent was gentle and graceful, like a dance that knows no gravity.

She woke with a start. The room was dark, and the air was warm and damply humid, yet she felt cold, chilled. Outside, the rain still fell, the torrential outburst of earlier had softened into a misty drizzle. Then she saw Ceriful in front of the window. He was still like a statue except for the powerful wings that beat slowly, a steady ominous rhythm. She felt disbelief. How could he be there? Why was he there?

She ran from her room and tore down the corridor; there was a door that she knew took her up to the big tower at the very top. She found it, quietly unlocked it, and inside the spiral staircase she went up and up, until she was in a room that offered a 360 degree view of the coast, like some sort of lighthouse without the light. She walked out onto the circular balcony where he now stood.

"Ceriful," she called out his name.

She heard no response. Why was he silent? Why didn't he speak? What had she done wrong? She could see his black horn spiralling out from his forehead. It seemed to swallow up the darkness, becoming blacker and blacker.

"Ceriful?"

Nothing, only eerie silence. Ceriful lowered his head. The horn was levelled at her; it split the air between them with a dreadful certainty. Raven felt an awful sadness. She began walking towards him, becoming aware that it was raining; a gentle misty type of rain, strangely comforting, she felt it on her face almost like kisses. As she came closer, she could see the drops that had collected on his coat and sparkled on his mane like crystal tears. She stopped only when she felt the cold tip of his horn touch her throat. She couldn't see it except as a sliver of night that was darker than the surrounding space; she could feel the infinite iciness that emanated from its depths. The tip was poised against the hollow of her throat; her pulse beat against it like a moth trapped beneath a silver needle, and it beat strong and loud.

One small step – only one would be needed and the black blade would pierce her skin, and her blood would run down its glacial shaft.

His voice flowed through her like some wonderful elixir. The pressure against her neck was lifted, and she felt his soft skin brush past her face and the angel from her dream was standing there; his wings covering her. His lips were pressed against her lips and she felt herself falling, falling into a place that was suddenly very familiar, and unexpectedly everything became incredibly clear.

Chapter Nineteen

$\mathbf{H}$alo visited the online bars in one of the border zones that intersected where the normals cruised, and where the dark illicit web began. Five bars later, he found her. He watched and waited, just to make sure but in the end, it was she that came over. Her persona was a white lighthouse with a beacon that flashed blue light every two seconds.

"I wouldn't have thought this was your type of place," she said.

Halo wasn't sure what sort of place this was, the vibe was certainly unusual but that didn't really give much away. "I was looking for you." Halo replied.

"Best get a private booth then," she said, turning and signalling so one of the staff came over and took them through a few rooms until they were sitting in a cage where black-leafed vines rapidly grew up and over until, within seconds, they were completely enclosed in rustling vegetation, and except for the flashing of her light beacon, they were in darkness.

Jo discarded her avatar and sat there as a holographic version of herself. She clicked her finger and small lanterns grew from the leafy walls and created a soft glow. Halo followed suit and wondered if he had enough credits to pay for this.

"Don't worry. I get good rates here. Now what is it you want to ask me?"

Halo broke away from studying the 3D version of her, which was incredibly detailed.

"I had some questions about Raven? Are you able to talk to me, or should I go through your friend?"

"I'm presuming she hasn't contacted Connor yet, and that you know where she is now."

"She's living in a place that belongs to her late father."

"Connor thought that must be where she is," Jo said. "Those people have their tentacles everywhere for them to have moved so fast to get her." She studied him. "Ask, and I'll see if I can answer?"

Halo hesitated a moment. "How did her mother die?"

"Did she ask you to come?" Jo stared at him. Her gaze was unsettling.

"No," he admitted.

"Are you going to tell her?"

"Probably."

"You care about her, I can see that," Jo said. Some drinks arrived, the goblets being carried over to them by two thick tendrils that grew from the bushy wall. As Jo touched the silver goblet the tendril opened up. She passed it to Halo and took one for herself.

Halo looked down into the swirling greenish black liquid.

"It will give you a light buzz," she said.

He took a sip; he had always found imbuing food online a disappointing experience. This drink surprised him by its thick luscious flavours, which seemed to burst onto his tongue. Perhaps he'd been going to the wrong places.

"It's also a mild aphrodisiac, I should mention that too," she laughed.

He wondered exactly what sort of bar it was.

"Are you in love with her?"

The question caught him by surprise.

"What's it to you?"

"Just wondering what motivates you."

"Does it matter?"

"Everything matters," she said quietly, "especially motivation."

"I'm concerned about her," he finally said.

"Is she your project? The little lost soul that you are impelled to save."

He took another sip. He was starting to feel irritated by her questions.

"Is that what the gargoyle is to you?" he asked.

She laughed. "Touché." She took a sip of her drink and put it down on a small leafy table that had just grown beside her.

"Ok you want to know how her mother died. She was murdered. Do you want the gory details?"

He thought for a moment before nodding.

"Her belly was cut open and her almost full term baby, Raven, was ripped out and the mother was left to bleed to death," her tone was matter of fact. She watched his reaction.

"It was a very brutal death. Are you going to tell her?"

"Probably not," Halo said. "Were there no suspects?"

"We're pretty sure we know who organised it. He, of course, didn't get his hands dirty, so it's a hard one to prove. Who actually did the deed? A paid killer no doubt; these people tend to melt away. They are professional and don't leave incriminating evidence."

"Why do that to the mother?"

"I think the word that was used was expediency. Of course, what they lost was their prize; she disappeared for sixteen years. I think you can assume her life – though poorer where she was – may well have been an improvement on what it would've been like with them."

"But now she is with them?"

"In two years, she can legally apply for her inheritance and walk away, as long as they haven't lured her to their way of thinking."

"Is that what they will do?"

"I'm guessing," Jo stared at him. "The world is a hard and cruel place. Raven has probably more of an idea of that than someone like you from a more privileged background. And don't spin me your story about growing up on a hippie commune. Your parents were still well off there compared to those living in the border communities or the closed zones," Jo looked at him. "Growing up a Carnie is a lesson in reality. I doubt she would want to go back despite the emotional bonds she may have with some of them."

Halo took another sip of his drink. He was starting to feel the effect, a strange warming sensation that was curling up his toes and into his legs.

"They are rich and powerful, and whatever gifts she has, they will want to utilise them. In some ways, it will not feel that different to where she was, except she will have more luxuries than she has ever thought possible."

Halo didn't say anything – everything he knew about Raven made him think that she couldn't be bought so easily, but did he really know that?

The warming sensation was moving up his legs and into his groin; he had never experienced anything like this before. Whatever it was, it wasn't mild. He was finding it hard to think about anything except that Jo really was one of the most extraordinary looking women he had ever seen.

"It will pass. What you are feeling," she said. "I suggest you just let it flow through you rather than attempt to do anything about it."

"Am I that transparent?" he asked.

"No, you are holding it better than many much older men that I've seen."

"What sort of bar is this?" he asked.

She laughed. Whatever she had been wearing had now dissolved into something like a second skin; it moulded her body, glowing in shades of silver and mauve. He dropped his goblet and moved towards her. He leaned in and felt her mouth against his; her body was now pressed up against him. He moaned. Her voice whispered something in his ear that sounded like; "This won't hurt a bit." Then her hands were stroking his hair, and her fingers were like ice as they probed his scalp, and freezing liquid began to ooze into him.

Shit, a mind fuck. Why did I not see this coming? Halo thought as he realised what was happening.

His lower body was burning while his mind was frosting up. The iciness was seeping through his head, into his brain. He knew enough to know that there was no point in fighting it, but he did anyway. The pain as the ice flowed into him was intense; he had not ever felt anything like this. He couldn't think anymore, his world had turned to a freezer zone, cold, white and Arctic. He was pressed against her, her body was like quicksand; it was sucking his body – his heat, and even his thoughts – they rolled back into her, and with it, memories flickered around him like an old projector movie turning on and off.

Suddenly everything beneath them collapsed, and the two of them fell, plummeting down a hole that seemed to continue into infinity, their bodies twisting and turning and hurtling on and on.

***

"Wake up, sleeping beauty," he heard her voice and opened his eyes. The gargoyle and Jo were standing over him.

"You," he said loudly. He tried to rise, but failed.

"Yes, it's me who came in and pulled you out before that creature really got her icy claws into you."

"That wasn't you?"

"No, just a pretender. A fairly good copy, I must say." She squatted down beside him and helped pull him up, so he was sitting leaning against the couch. His head was spinning. "Here, drink this. Black coffee, very strong. It will help clear your head."

He took a sip. It was lukewarm, bitter, and almost thick like syrup.

"I saw her trailing you as you came in. I suspect she'd been following you for a while."

"I must have detected you, but zeroed in on the wrong person."

"A lighthouse, as if I would use that." Jo said, "you know they are a warning to keep away, not to go sailing towards."

He looked a bit crushed.

"You did well to get that close to me," she said.

"And then I just turned into mush."

"You were pumped full of a rather heavy-duty aphrodisiac. Online or not, that program releases all sorts of neurotransmitters which work on the mind and effect the brain, regardless," she replied kindly, before laughing, "I must say, I found her pretty irresistible, myself."

"So, who was she?"

"Someone who was pumping you for information and wanted to give you a memory swipe, by the looks of it." Connor said.

Halo looked over at where Connor sat.

"What did the two of you talk about?" Connor said.

"I asked how Raven's mother died."

"What did she say?"

"That she was murdered, that her belly was sliced open, and the baby taken. Is that what happened?"

Connor nodded, "that is true. What else did you talk about?"

"She asked me a lot of questions," Halo said. "She seemed very interested in my relationship with Raven."

"That's probably what they wanted to find out, and that may have been the memories that they were planning to remove."

"Can they be that specific?" he asked.

"Not really, but if they do a swipe for the past few weeks that usually does the trick," Jo said. "Subliminal manipulation and subconscious hypnosis are one of the dirty secrets that many people are unaware can happen online. There are laws against their use, but that doesn't stop it from happening."

"Who are they?"

"The Institute that controls her father's legacy, I suspect," Connor replied.

Halo stood up and looked around the room. "How did you get in?"

"A few little locks don't stop anyone determined to get in, you should know that Halo."

"You got here fast."

"You've been out cold for at least two hours," Jo said, laughing.

"After she pulled you out, she had to track me down and we had to get here." Connor said.

"How did you get me out?" his last coherent thought had been of falling like some frozen corpse entwined with its nemesis.

"I had to dismantle the holographic floor under you. Those places are impossible to get into any other way, but you can come in from underneath, just start dismantling some code and the whole thing falls eventually, it's their only weak spot."

"I'm presuming Raven doesn't want to talk to me?" Connor interrupted.

"It's not personal," Halo sat down at the table across from Connor. "How big is this Institute?"

"Huge. It's really a corporation, but it's run privately so there is very little information. The Heimdallr Institute. The director is a man called Mars Lodstrom, a boyhood friend of her father. He has been chairman for the past sixteen years and is pretty much the head. What he says goes, it seems."

"What do you know about remote viewing?" Halo asked.

"Because her mother Junko Takara was a remote viewer, that was her name by the way," Connor's look made him feel ashamed for not asking that. "I know a bit," Connor continued. "She was apparently quite unique, it is still a rather secretive field, but we do know the Institute employs a few. Is Raven showing skills in that area?"

"Maybe," he replied. He looked at them both; he needed to talk to someone about his and Raven's experiences online. Jo, seemed savvy enough, and Connor struck him as more open minded than most. He began to tell them about the slipstream; trying to describe what it was like, how different it was to anything else online, and even how they accessed it, which was a hard one as he often wasn't sure how he did. It was almost like once they decided to be there, they were there. Saying those words out loud made him wonder about his sanity, but neither Jo nor Connor reacted to what he was saying as being particularly crazy.

"I have a feeling I've heard something that sounds similar; I'll see what I can find out," said Jo thoughtfully after he had finished. "And Raven accesses it remotely, you say. Now that is very interesting."

"Do you think this Institute might have something to do with the slipstream?" Halo asked.

Jo shrugged, "it's possible." She passed him over a small wafer connected to a jewel-like stud. "Here, use this if you need to contact me. It's much faster than bar hopping."

She glanced over at Connor, whose face was impassive, but Jo could feel the emotions that he was keeping well hidden.

Connor reached into his pocket and passed something to Halo; a chain on which hung two pendants. One was a flat crystal and paper-thin. It was etched with markings; a five-pointed star within a circle within a cross within a flaming comet. The other was a hologram crystal, shining with multi-fractured laser lights that pierced the area around it with blue and green prisms.

"This belonged to her mother. I should keep it for evidence, but…" he stopped and sighed. "Give it to her next time you see her. She should have it."

Only Jo knew how much that cost him to part with. She placed a hand on his shoulder.

"We should go," he said, standing up.

Connor had walked to the door and was waiting there. Jo was standing. "Just give me a minute," she called and then leaned down towards Halo.

"Halo, I know it must be hard for Raven to trust a policeman, but Connor is more than that. In this world where many people are ruthless, hard, and totally selfish, it's rare to meet someone like him. He is a good man. It would mean a lot to him if she contacted him, it really would. This has been a cold case that he has never given up on."

Halo picked up the chain and looked at it. "I'll give it to her. And if and when I see her again, I'll try to convince her to call him."

Chapter Twenty

On New Year's Day
I long to meet my parents
as they were before my birth.

Natsume Sōseki

The Past

To you, my darling daughter, as yet unnamed, my sweet one, who right at this moment is doing somersaults inside my belly. Well, that is what it feels like. I want to tell you my story, or at least part of it, the important parts. I want you to understand me and my past, and also your father. So, I shall start right at the beginning.

I grew up in a castle on a small island in the middle of the Seto Inland Sea in Japan. There, my father was revered as a prophet, and my mother as the beautiful exotic foreigner that had intoxicated him, as my favourite aunt would tell me. I entered the world just as an earthquake shook our tiny isle. This seemed to be viewed as something special, or something ominous. I'm still unsure which it was, perhaps both.

My father always said that yin and yang were more about complimentary and interconnectedness, rather than the duality of opposites. My world until I was seven was as wonderful as any childhood could be; I spent most of my days running through the forests, climbing the ancient pine trees, swimming in the warm waters that surrounded my island, and were home to a myriad of fish and porpoises. I saw the spirits – the Kami – the sacred spirits that appear as wind, rain, mountains, trees, rivers, and lakes, they were all around me, they were my childhood friends. To me, they were as real as the boats that came by daily with our supplies, and I was never told that it was my imagination; my father in particular told me that they were indeed real, and I would learn many important messages from them.

My home wasn't really a castle, but it seemed that way to me; it was far bigger than a normal house and it was a place where people would come to meditate and heal themselves and discuss spiritual ways that would help the earth heal.

I was surrounded by so much love; not just my father and mother, but all these aunts and uncles around me who spoiled me. Then something huge happened and maybe more terrible because what occurred was shrouded in mystery. My mother and father and Aunt Kimiko – my father's oldest and most trusted friend – had gone to one of the holiest mountains in Japan, Mount Hakusan, to watch the summer Solstice sunrise. They weren't alone, they were with two guides and at least twenty other people who had also made the trek up to the peak that morning. But somewhere between the sunrise, which was live streamed onto their website, and their descent they disappeared. Just… disappeared. There were searches that went on for weeks; looking for them, then looking for their bodies, searching for anything, trying to find some clue. Nothing was found. The two guides had gone ahead of them and were at the chalet organising their lunch. Many of the other walkers remembered seeing them, speaking to them even, but at some point, they just disappeared.

Their disappearance would not have been so dramatic if my father wasn't the head of a religious sect that had, at one time, been linked to a Christian organisation called the Pacific Rim Rapturists. Although his religious sect was not in any way Christian, there were some mystical teachings within it that added some extra credence. Within the 'The Way of The Wave' – that was the name of his group – it was like a bomb was detonated. Many believed he and his wife, and his first disciple Kimiko had ascended into heaven or more correctly had ascended to meet with Christ in the air, and to help bring about the second coming of Christ. I wasn't that aware of this at the time, this was my mother and father and favourite aunt, and I didn't understand what had happened except that they were gone. I felt such overwhelming sadness and distress. But the schism within the group was huge, and it played out in the media in a grotesque way.

My grandmother, Aoi had come to the island to look after me, she had also brought lawyers to work out the intricate details of my inheritance, and what belonged to my father's organisation. Much of this I learned about later when I was older, but one particular horrible event I will never forget. There was an interview with a media group that was being broadcast, the Anti-Rapture side had brought me along to the interview to prove their position, and I was asked a question about my father. I was confused and crying, and said the opposite, which of course started the Pro-Rapturists into a riot of praying and singing, and they dragged me physically over to their side. Suddenly, both groups were pulling me by my arms from one side to the other. I was screaming, and then someone actually pulled my shoulder out from its socket. I was in agony, and writhing on the ground, which the Rapture group took as a sign to do the same. I don't remember that much, except someone realised what was going on, and called an ambulance.

My grandmother was so furious, she had been in talks with lawyers about my father's will and the different legal trusts set up and had thought that I was being looked after. She called in a security firm, threw everyone off the island, and set up surveillance, so no one could enter. She also did something similar to the Oshiba property – cutting it in half with a line of armed guards and making all who were there choose which faction they stood with. Many left, but many stayed.

After I was discharged from hospital, she took me home to their family estate and my dear Aunt Riku – my father's sister – took on the day-to-day care of me. But I was ripped away from my island home and that was terrible, I missed it so much, it was a severance that I'm not sure I've ever really gotten over. I did visit it various times over the years, but it was never again my home; something that Sebastian and I had hoped to change. Now that I am legally the owner, we were hoping to make that our home – a place for ourselves and our children; beginning with you, my darling.

The island was separate from the other properties; part of a private trust that was shared equally between my father, my mother, Kimiko, and me. It was seven years after their disappearance that they were declared legally dead, and then inheritance tax needed to be paid, but my grandmother being aware of all of that, had prepared. The Way of the Wave organisation she left with lawyers, and after much legal wrangling she took control of my father's books and documents, which she claimed belonged to him privately. Most of that is locked on the island in his library and study. All of the memories of this have come flooding back because I feel like I'm in a similar situation again with what is happening with your father's estate, only this time I'm an adult, and do not have the formidable aid of my grandmother and her legal team. I struggle to understand what I am entitled to, and what I need to be fighting for. If it was just I, I would probably not care. But, I want you to know your father, to understand what he was working towards, and what he believed in.

I feel I have moved away from what I really want to tell you, of course, my wish is you will never need to see this, or that we will watch it together one day and laugh.

Takara pressed pause and took a deep breath. She had a sip of the cold tea sitting beside her; she stared across at the camera pointing at her, the green light blinking like one of the beacons on the dark sea around her island warning of shallow water. Warning of danger.

She pressed record.

After moving in with my grandmother and my Aunt Riku – which was a huge change, although they tried very hard to make me feel comfortable, they gave me my father's old bedroom and studio, and because the move had been so sudden, I was able to choose how I wanted it painted and decorated. I loved his studio, much of what he owned I kept as treasured items, and most of my belongings from my bedroom on the island were brought over, as well as things from my parent's bedroom and our private rooms, and of course my beloved pets, the two cats, a goat and donkey. So, I can't say that life was terrible there; it wasn't, but I was very sad for a long time, and I struggled to be part of this world that seemed very unfamiliar to me.

I also had no one to talk to me about my other abilities; my father had always been the one I spoke to about how I could see or feel the spirits around me. How I could fall into a trance and be somewhere totally different, and see people and hear them talking, how many of my dreams weren't dreams but something else entirely, many were prophetic – something I didn't understand for a long time. I ended up not talking about any of it and trying to ignore it, which will only work for a certain amount of time.

How I actually found my way was quite unexpected. I was at the lawyers with my grandmother and Aunt; there may have been documents that I needed to sign; I can't remember now, I was about fourteen and sitting on a couch near a window, doing some homework. All the adults were at a large table talking about the two factions of my father's organisation that were fighting for the right to use his name. I wasn't consciously listening and maybe I was tired, as I started falling asleep. I found myself in an unfamiliar room listening to a similar conversation but with different people, I realised that this was one of the groups and they were discussing us. I don't know what I heard, but I got up and walked over to the table and began repeating what I was hearing. I opened my eyes to all these surprised adults staring at me, but what I said must've made sense as they all began talking about it. I felt very embarrassed and weird and went back to my seat.

One of the men came over, he introduced himself to me, although I don't recall his name, but he quietly told me that I had given them some very important information, and that what I had just done was called Remote Viewing. He asked me if he could visit me at my home and bring some people that would be able to help me. And that was how I began to do what I do and which ultimately brought me into contact with Sebastian.

Sebastian, your father, how can I even describe him to you? Describe his essence; describe what compelled him, how he thought, what he wanted to do, and his vision. I can talk about how he looked. His dark hair and his deep green eyes, that were the colour of the conifers of my island, I remember thinking that, when I first looked into them. He had a thin face, an intense face even, and he had this way of being almost motionless, I don't know how exactly to describe it, my father had that similar quality as well, it was as though they walked within their own space, somehow apart from others. Like my father when Sebastian spoke, the words seemed to have arisen from deep within, and were important. Distilled from the depths and alchemised upwards.

He was tall and thin, yet had an elegance that reminded me of another time, another century. He was courteous and thoughtful, attributes so missing in our brash present day, belonging to the past, this was his persona, but oh his mind. His mind belonged to the future; his mind travelled somewhere far out there into a universe that didn't exist yet. That was how I perceived him. He had five academic degrees, had been some sort of child prodigy, at university when he was fourteen, and by the time he was twenty-five, he had finished degrees in biochemistry, geophysics, artificial intelligence, genetics, and bioethics. He was thirty-two when we met, and he had begun implementing these research programs that – to me at least – seemed mind-blowing. He had a vast network of scientists clamouring to work with him, and funds; his company was awash with sponsorships and grants; private and government; and I have to admit that was Mars's doing. That was what he bought into their organisation – Mars was part bully, part salesmen, an immoral spruiker, imposing and intimidating, and yet he could somehow sell the vision, make businessmen believe that they needed to be involved, that if they didn't, they would regret it for the rest of their life.

Mars and Sebastian, so different and so intertwined, they were like brothers, more than brothers; they had been best friends since they were five, yet I struggled to understand this bond that ensnared them. I struggled to understand Mars and his hold on Sebastian. And why he seemed to dislike me so much; hate me almost. Even now, when we both have lost this man that we have so loved, when we should've been united by our grief. It is almost the opposite, he hides his malice behind a cool civility, only that I am carrying Sebastian's baby, I suspect holds the worst of his feelings back. I don't want to speak any more about Mars; it's your father I want to tell you about.

I dreamed about him before I knew anything at all about him; a very vivid and realistic dream. I was watching him walk through the huge auditorium of a conference centre, he was surrounded by people. He was led through these back labyrinth-like corridors into another large room, with more people surrounding him. Then more movement, more corridors, more rooms, more people. And suddenly he was alone, on a dark stage, with a spotlight shining a beam of light that pooled at his feet. And in that moment, I knew he was going to die, and that's when I woke up. I dreamt the same dream the following night and again woke up filled with dread. Who was this man, I wondered?

A few hours later I knew; I was doing a transcript of a previous viewing, I had already submitted my verbal report, but they wanted a detailed written one. I decided I needed a break and switched screens and caught an interview on one of the news channels. I was about to click to something else when his face appeared. So, I sat and listened to him talk, listened to his ideas, new ways we could live that would help us, all of us with the climactic changes that had begun. His words entranced me, the clarity of his ideas and, of course, my dreams added an extra edge. I searched for more about him and found so much, that I was going to be swamped if I read it all. I quickly finished the transcript and sent it off. I knew I needed to work out what would be the best strategy to avert what was going to happen.

I flew to the city where he was the principal speaker at a big conference; I arrived on the day not knowing how I was going to see him, or even talk to him. There were no tickets available, and the security was immense. I walked through the park that circled this centre and saw a beautiful Japanese maple tree just beginning to turn crimson. I sat on the grass below it and asked the Kami to help me. I closed my eyes, and just let myself connect to the earth and this beautiful tree that I was leaning on. I don't know how long I sat there, I felt a leaf flutter down, brush past my face and land in my lap. A scarlet star with seven points lay on my black jumper. I stood up and placed the leaf in my pocket and began walking, a wind had blown up and was swirling the fallen leaves from the trees along this avenue I walked. Leaves were blowing around me and against my clothing. I stopped and leaned over and, amid the crackling leaves, my fingers picked up a folded piece of cardboard. It was a ticket to the conference, door six, and the admission time was now. I thanked the spirits and walked around until I found the right door and then swiped my ticket under the laser light and walked in.

How to find this man, this Sebastian Van Elson, who would no doubt be surrounded by so many people, security as well, and who was I? I had no clearance to be anywhere but inside the conference centre, sitting in the seat the ticket had allocated. I trusted that I would find him, after all the dreams had come to me, the ticket had literally blown into my hand, I was here for a reason. I walked along darkened corridors that ended at a wall of elevators. I waited, didn't touch the buttons, trusted. One of the elevators stopped, it was empty, but I walked into it, the doors closed, and I felt it rise. When it stopped, the doors opened, and a man walked in, he was facing away from me, calling back to someone still in the hallway. The doors closed and he moved against the wall and looked at me.

For a few seconds, we both stared at each other; the elevator was still going up, I wasn't sure if he had even pressed the button. I needed to say something. I felt the small jolt beneath my feet. We had stopped. As the doors began to open, he gave me a slight smile and I reacted by leaning forward and touching the sleeve of his jacket.

"Please, I need to talk to you," I blurted out. "You don't know me, but it's important."

"Better follow me then," he replied as we both stepped out into the dimly lit lobby. "Do you like tea?"

Across this small lobby, we walked, and he flicked his wrist under a light lock, and the door opened to a medium-sized room with lounge chairs and a table that could seat eight people, and a kitchenette that ran along one wall. The other wall was floor-to-ceiling glass, overlooking the surrounding parkland and city.

"Tell me your name and take a seat. I'll make us some tea; I tend to go for a green tea at this time of the afternoon. Does that suit you?"

"Yes," I replied. "Takara, my name is Takara Takenaka."

"I shall make us a Japanese green tea, with ginger and lotus. Does that suit? You are Japanese?" He had switched to speaking in Japanese to me.

That was how I met your father. Over the next half hour, I told him why I had been impelled to find him, I told him of my dreams, the three recurring dreams. I told him I was a remote viewer and I remember telling him I was not mad or crazy and that made him laugh. As I spoke, his phone kept pinging him messages, and even a few calls came in which he didn't take, although he scanned the messages as I spoke. Just as I finished speaking, an alarm sounded throughout the building and an immense figure pushed the door opened and strode in.

"Why the fuck haven't you taken my calls? There's a major security breach."

The man looked at me, grabbed my arm and hauled me up from the couch, practically lifting me in the air.

"Mars. What are you doing? She is my guest."

That was how I met Mars. He let me go roughly so I fell back onto the couch, my head hitting the backrest, my arm aching, as it was the same one that had been dislocated from my shoulder when I was a child. Sebastian sat next to me, asking if I was all right and staring at Mars and telling him, that I was a better source of security information than our security. This didn't go down well. Mars accused me of being an agent and possibly the assassin herself, he wanted to strip-search me for potential weapons that might be on me and interrogate me. Meanwhile another man had entered the room and interrupted this very heated exchange between Sebastian and Mars, to say we needed to leave as the conference centre was in lockdown. Sebastian insisted I leave with him in his car; the whole evening was a blur, neither Sebastian nor I found out until the next day how close he was to being killed, and that it was me being in his room talking to him that probably saved him. He was supposed to have left ten minutes earlier to go downstairs to one of the secure rooms that would lead him up onto the stage.

I stayed at Sebastian's hotel suite that night, and for the next few nights, I stayed in one of the extra rooms, but each night when we were alone we talked and talked until the early hours. By the time we both flew back here, he had not only asked me to come and work for him, but had told me he was in love with me, and asked me if I would marry him? I didn't say yes to any of those offers for another few months, but even when he asked me, I knew I would say yes; somehow it was our fate, our destiny. I don't know, but something stronger than either of us was orchestrating this. This city is my mother's hometown; when I made the decision to move here, it had been a mix of curiosity and just needing to get away to a place where no one knew anything about me. I didn't know that this man had also moved here for different reasons, and made this city not just his home, but also the world headquarters of the Heimdallr Institute."

Takara stopped, she felt overwhelmed by the memories, her emotions, her grief. To have met this wonderful man, to have loved and been loved back with such intensity, to be given this gift of a baby and then to have him so cruelly taken from her, it was almost unbearable. She looked at her hands on the desk; they looked so tiny and frail, she willed her right hand to move over to the button and press stop. She didn't want to be filmed with the tears running down her face and plopping onto the desk – to be filmed with her mouth crying out with the pain, this unbearable pain. She let herself surrender and cry until she couldn't cry any longer.

She took a deep breath, it was asking too much for her to tell her story in one sitting; it would take more than one, but she would send this one now, that was important too. She plugged in the device Riku had sent her. It was a type of encryption device and with it she could log in as a different identity to one of the various aliases that had been set up for her. She quickly set up the different tags that would send this recording off safely. She pressed the microphone on and began speaking Japanese.

My beloved Aunt Riku, I'm sending this video recording to you for safe keeping, just in case. I know you will hold onto it. If something should happen to me, when my daughter is older, please find a way to give it to her. I know you are going to suddenly feel very worried about me, please don't. It's just a precaution, and I'm aware because of my childhood how quickly the unexpected can happen. Once again, I need to tell you of my love and endless gratitude to you for taking care of me for so many years. I know you thought me strange, and probably still do; I know you don't understand the gifts I have. But I know that you have loved me regardless, as you did your brother, my father. Your kindness and wisdom were anchors for me through all the turbulence. And as you see, still is.

Since losing Sebastian, I feel very alone and vulnerable. I wish I could come home and have my baby there; in my dreams, I walk my island and think that if I could give birth to her there, all would be well. Again, I'm sure my words are filling you with dread, please everything is fine here. There are so many legal papers I need to sign, so many strange concepts regarding Sebastian's company that I need to understand. And you know I'm not terribly good at all that. I feel I'm stuck once again in that confusing, bizarre place where I'm somehow intrinsic to an organisation that I have no real personal validity and connection to. When I was a child, it was to my father's religious sect, which of course was in total disarray after my parents' disappearance, and where I was pulled to and fro between the splintered groups. Now it is to my husband's organisation; it is not so much splintered because it is held in the vicelike grip of Sebastian's business partner, Mars. He is so different to Sebastian, and yet together they created this institute in the hope that through science, they would be able to bring the world back from the brink of climate catastrophe. I don't trust Mars, I know he has an agenda that I can't see or understand. I know that these words will worry you. Please, don't. I will call you in a few days and we can have a long talk then. This is only sent as a precaution.

On a happier note, my daughter is due to be born on the day of the eighth full moon of the year. Yes, the Tsukimi moon. How I loved those autumn moon festivals when I was a child. I've been thinking of calling her Mizuki. Beautiful moon. And yes, you are going to so laugh at that, because you will remember my father's much loved, deep as midnight black cat, Mizuki. Thank you so much my beloved Aunt, please pass my love on to all the family, and we'll talk in the next few days.

Chapter Twenty-one

Oh what can ail thee, knight-at-arms,
Alone and palely loitering?
The sedge has withered from the lake,
and no birds sing.

John Keats

He stepped into the long black limousine and wondered if it would bring him back. He had left a message with Jo, he figured she would be less constrained by legalities, and she seemed like someone with a can-do approach. The windows were blackened but he focused on listening, they went through two checkpoints, which meant they were leaving the city.

One of the women from the other meeting met him in an underground car park and escorted him to a lift and then along a maze of corridors to a small courtyard with a very large oak tree where Raven was waiting at a small table. She was wearing a sundress that looked like a Monet painting, all greens and blues and dappled sunlight. The table was full of sandwiches and cupcakes, a veritable spread of nostalgic edibles like something from a child's story.

"Hello," he leaned towards her and kissed her cheek. "I was surprised when I got your message."

"You're the only person I trust."

"I have my uses then."

He reached over and poured himself a glass of what looked like fruit punch. He took a sip and gazed around the enclosure. Apart from the large oak tree, the rest of the vegetation was sparse, or maybe it was sculptured. It was hard to tell; he wasn't sure if the shapes he could see were flora or something entirely man-made. There was definitely man-made artwork against some of the walls, silver and glass and multicoloured spirals of steel. He looked at the buildings that sprawled behind the walls.

"That's where I live," she said as she pointed up to the top level, all glass and steel.

"Do I get to see?" he asked.

"Maybe," she smiled.

The air was surprisingly clean and fresh, and there was a salty tang to it. He looked up at the open sky and then over to the far wall, which was transparent. Through it, a wild sea was heaving and rolling.

"Do you want to go over and look?" she asked.

They walked across the small expanse, stood at the perimeter and looked out; the colours of the sea struck him intensely, so rich and alive; the deep green and midnight-blue swirls with the creamy coating of white foam.

"I haven't looked at the ocean for such a long time," he said. "The sea proper, not those tame places that they pretend are the sea but we all know are just enclosed versions." He breathed in the salty ozone scent, he felt it deep in his lungs and it made him feel more alive than he thought was possible.

"Our world is so fucked up," Halo said. "We breathe in toxins daily and we don't even realise how bad it is until we breathe in what the air should really be like." He looked around. "Why is it that these places are still closed off? They say it's unsafe, yet these people wouldn't be here if it was. They understand more than the rest of us what is safe and what is not. They advise the authorities on that and yet here they are in perfect isolation, keeping this all to themselves," he said. "Why is that? What else do they do out here, away from prying eyes?"

She shook her head; the breeze ruffled her hair so that strands from her fringe covered her eyes. "I met Mars Lodstrom," she said. "He runs the Heimdallr Institute. He came to introduce himself to me; he was an old friend of my father."

"What's he like?" Halo asked.

"Intimidating. But he did try to make me feel at ease," she said. "He spoke about all that the institute could do for me."

"What about what he expected in return?"

She looked puzzled.

"He must wonder what gifts you've inherited from your parents. He must be aware of your mother's remote viewing skills and wonder if you have skills like her," Halo said. "Did he say anything about your mother? Did you ask?"

She looked out at the sea; a hundred mermaids were cavorting in the swell, the scales on their fishy tails flashed in the sunlight like tiny mirrors. She could hear their singing too, melancholy and sad, yet somehow transcendental and elevating as well. She felt the urge to discard her dress and dive off the cliff and join them. Her fingers pushed into the Perspex wall until she wondered if they would start bleeding, she was pressing so hard.

She closed her eyes and tried to breathe.

"Raven," his voice, so full of concern, brought her back. "Are you all right?" he felt he was always asking her that question.

She nodded and began talking; her words were ragged and sharp and seemed to cut deep into her as she spoke.

"He told me how my mother had gone into labour early; there had been complications. The doctor who was assigned to her had performed an emergency caesarean in her apartment and it had not gone well. She died there on the floor, and he left, apparently to take me to the hospital, but then he was involved in an accident on the way. He was found dead in his car, but there was no sign of me. They've been looking for me ever since. Mars had various theories on how I ended up with the Carnies."

Halo decided not to tell her about what he had heard, he could sense she was upset already by what she had learned; would it help her knowing that it was not a tragic accident, but premeditated murder?

"Do you feel his intentions are sincere? Mars?" he asked quietly.

She looked out at the sea again and thought about what she had felt after he had left the room. He was such a big man, over six foot seven, with broad shoulders and even in his stylish suit there was something physically potent about him, and she had been scared. He looked like he could snap her neck with just one of his large hands. There was an aura of intensity about him, and she doubted that her wishes would make the slightest difference to what he wanted; he had some plan, and that plan would prevail no matter what she may want. She wondered if her mother had been frightened of him.

"I don't know," she finally said.

She gazed into his eyes. Halo felt himself falling into their grey-green depths. He felt himself sinking into some strange world just below the surface of reality. He didn't believe her. She was holding back a lot, he could tell; he knew in his bones that there was much she hadn't said, but as he looked into her eyes, the truth began to have less meaning as he sank further down into their depths. He felt like he was going to pass out. He pulled his gaze from her. He looked instead down into the swell of the waves, rising twenty feet or so, as they came crashing into the cliffs below. There was less danger there than in her eyes.

Raven moved closer and he felt her fingers on his face, and then she was kissing him and he fell once more into that floating rapturous unreal world, and this time he didn't want to resurface. He finally was the one that pulled away.

"I have something for you," he said as he led her back to the table under the tree. When she was seated, he passed the chain over to her. "It belonged to your mother."

She took it and looked at the two pendants dangling from the chain. She looked like she might cry.

"The detective gave it to me, to give to you."

"Was she wearing this when…?"

"I'm guessing she was."

She wrapped her fingers around it, brought it to her chest, and closed her eyes.

It felt wrong to watch her at this time. This was a private moment; he couldn't even begin to understand what it must be like for her to grow up not knowing anything about her parents and then suddenly be faced with the reality of their deaths.

He looked up at the leaves of the enormous tree; from where he was sitting, all he could see was leaves – the sky was totally hidden. Here the light was a greenish gold and gentle on the eye while all around the harsh white walls of the buildings were dazzlingly bright in the glaring sunlight. He blinked and felt incredibly tired. He closed his eyes for a moment and felt himself falling, falling, and falling.

Around him the trees spun by in blurry muted browns and greens, his horse's hooves thundered on the forest floor. The trees, oak, elm, larch, birch whizzed by as branches snapped in his wake, his armour clanged against his body, reassuring him with its weight and familiarity. His horse snorted and around him the hounds bayed loudly, a frenzied howling as though they were possessed. All birdsong had long ago faded before the hunt, and from behind came other riders and the fleet footed archers with their bows and arrows. Ahead, he could discern a white shape – their quarry — weaving in and out of the trees and ferns. On and on they ran, yet the distance between hunter and hunted didn't change. This improbable beast that he was hunting and, for the briefest moment, he wondered who was leading whom? Was he the hunter, or was he the hunted? Around him, the trees seemed to move like a living chessboard; surrounding him, disorienting him, cutting him off from the others so it was only him on his horse, and the white elusive beast that ran ahead. And far behind him – an endless distance behind – sat a young woman, waiting, waiting for the hunt to be over.

But whom was she really waiting for? Him? Or the magical beast he pursued?

Raven's voice reeled him back from the endless forest that had once encompassed the globe. He blinked and was back under the tree in the cool light with the salty wind blowing his hair.

"Would you thank the detective for me?" she asked.

"Of course."

"Would you help me put it on?"

He stood up, walked behind her, and took the chain in his hands. He undid the clasp and then redid it at the base of her neck. He placed his hands on her shoulder for a brief moment and felt the warmth of her skin against his palms. Her scent rose up, deliciously delicate and sweet. He wanted to kiss her neck, her shoulders; he took a deep breath, lifted his hands, and walked back to his seat.

"Someone else came to see me," she said. "Azûrâ. With her father."

"Azûrâ?"

"Yes, I'm not sure who was more surprised," Raven replied. "There is a small party being planned for me. Azûrâ is to sing there. I think her father is part of this organisation. I think they were hoping we might become friends." She looked at Halo. "Are you still seeing her?"

"I haven't seen her for quite a few weeks. Am I invited to the party?"

"Of course. I've given your name to the organiser, you should receive your invite soon."

"Would you mind also organising an invitation for someone else?" Halo said, thinking this might be a way for Jo and Connor to at least see her. "Her name is Jo, I think she is someone you should meet."

Raven stared at him for a moment, she wanted to ask him who this woman was but refrained. Secrets swirled around them; untidy and messy, like weeds coming up in the perfect lawn beneath their feet.

"Give me her details and I'll put her on the list," she finally said.

She picked up a plate of sandwiches and offered it to him. He took one and ate it as she did. Suddenly, there was an uncomfortable silence between them.

She topped up his glass, poured herself a drink and looked up at the building behind her; at the glass that hid her living quarters, and to the tower that rose up like some strange lighthouse without a light.

"Halo, do you trust me?" she asked. "I mean, if I made a decision, would you accept I had my reasons and that it was something I needed to do?"

Halo looked at her. "Is this something to do with the slipstream?"

"I can't say. I just may need to do something, sometime soon. And I won't be able to involve you, well not straight away," she knew she wasn't being very clear; well, how could she when she wasn't even sure what she was planning.

"It's not safe there. Shouldn't this be something we do together?" he asked.

"Halo, I need to know that when the time comes, you will know that I have my reasons. No matter what it may look like to you."

He reached over and took one of her hands. "Don't shut me out."

"Believe me I don't want to," she said. She took a deep breath, "but I will share this with you."

"I don't think Mars knew much about what I was doing with the Carnies, because if he did, he would've put in much more security." As she spoke, her entire face lit up with a big smile. "I think he thinks I just shop online or something, but I have all this time, and there is no one really here but me and my minders. There is a contingent of security staff, but they are pretty bored and it's easy to get info out of them; and why wouldn't they tell me, all this supposedly belongs to me. Or will in two years. Those buildings over there, inside is a massive supercomputer, seriously," she paused, "there are a couple of shifts of IT staff that live on-site for two weeks before swapping with another crew. I think the penthouse where I am is rarely used; maybe for visiting scientists or important guests. And let me tell you, it took four hours to smash through their internal security and rewrite the portal going in so no one would suspect."

"I'm impressed. You are brilliant."

"Not brilliant, it wasn't exactly hard. A lot I still don't understand, and there is an awful amount of data flowing by, scientific research, meteorological and climate statistics; it's like it almost contains everything – and it does – it feeds out to other places, but really everything is contained here. I have managed to find out more information about my father, and also my mother; there are surveillance tapes of her, some of her and Sebastian, and some of just her. I suspect Mars organised those; there is a certain coded signature when there is stuff that belongs to him. And there is something really strange there, I don't know what it is, it is not like anything I've ever come across."

"Could it relate to the slipstream?"

"I don't think so. Whatever it is, its hyper-secure and has its own power source. The encryption is nothing like I've ever seen, or even remotely like any other form of encryption that I'm aware of. It's really different. I'll keep circling it. Something will eventually make sense."

"Be careful," he said.

"Always," she smiled.

"Can I help, you know I have certain skills in that area."

"But you'd need to be here, you wouldn't get through from the outside."

"You could always invite me to stay for a night or two," he smiled at her. "I promise I'll behave."

"I'll work on something," she replied. "Here come the minders. I'll get them to bring us coffee, got to keep them occupied so they don't start spying or listening to us."

Chapter Twenty-two

Deep in thought I sketch bamboo, clouds form in the ink stone;
In high spirits I paint orchids, fragrance fills the paper.
I add in raindrops suddenly startling the heron to flight,
I fill in the eyes instantly rousing the dragon from sleep.

Natsume Sōseki

The Past

The dream was so strikingly vivid that when Takara woke up it was almost like she was still standing in that moonlit pine forest, that she had blinked, opened her eyes and yet hadn't moved. The images of the three foxes were etched so clearly in her mind, two white ones and the flame red vixen. Above their heads flickered the strange flames called kitsunebi, the ghost lights, casting an eerie glow over their fur and ears. Their eyes shone like lanterns and within their depths she recognised their souls. She knew them, remembered them, and whispered their names.

She walked across the cool floors of her new apartment; unpacked boxes loomed like shadowy cliffs in the corners. She didn't like the apartment that much but it was out of the way and offered a high level of security. It was the lotus pond that had clinched the deal, the two bedrooms opened up onto their very own section of the pond with a small deck and walkway that curved its way around and over the pond. It was here she had found a sense of peace that had been missing since Sebastian's death. She wrapped the robe around her tightly and walked out onto the deck and slowly around the path that twisted like a figure eight. It was dawn and there was a mist rising from the water, swirling from beneath the huge circular leaves, the flowers were still tightly closed up and she could hear small splashes in the water, perhaps of frogs or the koi that called the pond home. For a moment she leaned on the railing and closed her eyes, feeling herself far away, long ago, with her parents, with Kimiko and some of the others. To a time where her entire world was cosseted with so much love and laughter, that she had no idea that there was a world where that was in short supply.

Feeling the coldness of the mist wrapping around like a cloak, she knew she shouldn't stay out much longer; she walked back to her room, hearing the sound of their paws padding on the wooden deck and then on the tiles. *They're here to stay*, she thought, *but why?*

She knew why, it was for the same reason she had moved here.

Kasei, Fire star. Mars.

Sipping the hot, green lotus-flower tea, she recalled that day so vividly, how long had she pestered Riku before her aunt finally agreed to take her. It was itself a convoluted journey. They had left early, just the two of them, and a basket packed with offerings, a jug of sake and handmade fried tofu sushi rolls. The drive took over an hour and that was just to where they parked the car. Takara was wearing her favourite hooded jacket, vermillion coloured with black fake fur trimming the hood. She wore a white jumper and dark green trousers. She recalled how long she had spent choosing what she would wear.

The path they took led them from the small village down into a meadow and then over a small bridge crossing a trickling stream where huge ferns cascaded down to the water. The way continued through a forest and then there was a fork in the road but it was obvious which path they needed to take, a faded red torii stood across one of the routes, this was the gateway to a Shinto shrine. The way led upwards, rough stairs were still visible among the ferns and overgrown shrubs. The large trees that reached upwards seemed to touch the heavy grey clouds, adding their dark shadows to the dim murky light, even though it was mid-morning, it seemed more like twilight. The path finally flattened out and they continued walking through the forest, Takara was wondering if they had somehow taken a wrong turn as the track was now so overgrown that to her eyes it didn't look like a path anymore.

The forest was thicker here too; the canopy was dense and the branches almost entwined together so barely any light filtered down to the fern strewn track, and she had reached out for her Aunt's hand, not daring to utter those words, how much longer, not after having asked for this. Riku had smiled down at her and squeezed her hand. She couldn't now remember how long it was, possibly only a matter of minutes before the path turned and there was the beginning of the avenue of torii gates, all weather-beaten, the once bright red paint now faded and cracked, a few almost decrepit and leaning over at an angle looking like they might just topple. The avenue continued on through the trees as they hurried along, her smaller legs going faster than her aunt's. Takara remembered how excited she had become when suddenly they had arrived, the Inari Shrine emerging out of the forest like some forgotten relic. At the entrance were two stone columns, on each sat a slender fox stature, guardians of the shrine.

Respectfully they both stopped at the stairs and bowed to these messengers of the Kami, one of them had a rolled up scroll in its month, the other a large key. As they climbed up, a priest came out of the shadows and they walked up to him. They both bowed.

Riku passed over the basket to him and he bowed and thanked them, he then pulled out a small wooden box from within his robes.

"Shake." He said as he passed it to the young girl.

Takara shook it and a small wooden stick fell out of the hole in the bottom. She bent over and picked it up. "Ichi." She said. She passed it back to the priest. He placed the stick on the wall next to one of the fox statures, and walked back down the stairs, they followed him as he led them behind the shrine and onto a path.

"Follow the path and in about five minutes you will come to the crossroads. You must wait beside the gate until a car, a person, an animal even, appears on the road. What arrives first is the key. Take notice of what it is, if it is a car, the colour, the type, the number plate and how many people are in the car. If it is a person, what they look like, their clothes, what are they carrying. Also which direction they are coming from and which road they choose. Then come back."

The forest encroached the crossroads from all sides. The cedars deep green and huge, they seemed to bend towards the road, it was now midday but it felt like the day was approaching evening. Together they waited beside the red gate. They waited and waited. Nothing appeared. It was eerily silent.

"How long do we wait?" she had finally asked.

"Till something appears," Her aunt replied.

Takara wondered how long that would be, what if nothing appeared, ever. Anxiety and fear began to grow inside her. What if there was no answer to her question?

"Something will come along, eventually," her aunt broke the silence.

Takara wasn't sure. She felt they were caught in some sort of time loop and maybe they would be here forever waiting. Maybe they had already been here for years and people were looking for them. Was this what had happened to her parents? Were they somewhere frozen in time, invisible to everyone?

"I think I hear something." Riku murmured. "Listen. Can you hear that too?"

Takara held her breath and listened; there was a faint sound, a humming sound, louder now, much louder in the few seconds of listening. Now it was definitely audible. An engine. Takara leaned over the gate and looked to her left, to where the sound was coming from and then it appeared. A black car was approaching, a very long black car. A limousine with tinted windows. It momentarily slowed down as it reached the intersection before it continued straight ahead and was lost to sight as the road curved around a bend. Takara watched the car disappear. She glanced back along the road it had come, staring at the asphalt that was suddenly spot lit by the sun that had come out between the clouds.

She heard Riku call her name and she turned reluctantly around.

The priest was waiting at the shrine, he smiled at them and asked Takara to first ask him the question she would like answered, and then proceed to tell him what she had seen.

Takara hesitated, she had waited so long to come here, to ask and now she wasn't sure. She felt so tired, exhausted after the long walk and then the long wait.

Finally, she took a deep breath and asked. "Will I see my parents again?"

The priest nodded, his eyes looked on her with kindness. "Now tell me what you saw, it was a long wait, you have been gone a while."

"Yes it was very long time, I thought it would not ever end," Takara replied. "The car that came was black. A long black limousine with the numbers 333 on the number plate, all of the windows were tinted, and it came from the south and headed straight ahead." She paused.

"Was there anything else?" The priest asked gently.

"After the car had disappeared and I looked back from where it had come, I saw…" She hesitated.

"Tell me what you saw, even if it seems insignificant or strange."

"I saw three foxes, they were sitting in the middle of the road. They were looking at me."

The priest smiled. "Three foxes are always a lucky omen." Then he became serious as he said, "Like your wait, I'm afraid to say it will be a long time before you see your parents again, I'm sorry to tell you that. You will meet them again, but it will not be here, do you understand what I'm saying? The foxes are a sign that you will meet them, but not in this world, in the otherworld. Perhaps you will be blessed to see them in a dream or even glimpse an aspect of them in a mirror or one night under the moonlight." He paused. "What colour were the foxes?"

"Two were white and one red." She replied.

He smiled again. "You are blessed to see them, I know my answer is not what you may have been hoping for, but this is a blessing none the less. Remember that the spirits are always close; I think you know that already. I think you have a great gift which over time will become apparent." He paused before saying, "I also think it would be a good idea if we made a picnic of these offerings, we will sit on the stairs and offer some to the guardians which will make them happy, and I know that they will want you to replenish yourself, there is still a long walk back."

He picked up the basket and they sat down on the stairs and shared the food, the sun came out as the clouds dispersed and Takara remembered how it seemed that the three foxes were scampering between the trees and every now and again she would see their foxy faces looking out at her. Yet despite her tiredness and the answer the priest had given her, she felt strangely peaceful.

Back in the car, Riku who had been quiet on the walk back, looked across at Takara. "I feel you are, perhaps not happy, but comforted by the answer to your question. You know there were many people who believed your mother was a kitsune, that she had bewitched your father, it was mainly the colour of her hair, but also her face with those pale green eyes." Riku laughed. "When we were children, Namiyo used to see foxes everywhere, he used to tell me they were kitsune. Some of them he claimed he had known through many lifetimes, he spun all these stories about them and him. I used to think he just had a wild imagination, but now I'm not so sure."

***

Takara leaned back in her chair and closed her eyes, thinking of her father and mother, memories drifting across her closed eyes, suddenly she felt movement within her extended belly, for a moment what was beneath her skin was rolling, undulating. She rubbed her large stomach and whispered, "my darling, you are awake now, and you are hungry, I'm hungry too. Suddenly I'm ravenously hungry." She wandered into the kitchen and prepared her breakfast, hearing the scampering of the fox's claws as they played between the boxes.

She began the arduous task of unpacking, sunlight filtered through the slats that shielded the windows and she spoke to the automated home monitoring system that opened the louvres more so the rooms were flooded with light.

She had been so shocked when Mars had come to Sebastian's apartment with three men and announced she would be moving to the spare apartment on the floor above.

Security, was Mars's reason, there was too much of Sebastian's notes and work here, this was very valuable, and it was worth a lot to other companies, competitors, he had said to her with that cold smile of his. Her new apartment was all fitted out with furniture and included a nursery for the baby, she would be comfortable and she was welcome to take what she needed. The study would be off limits but they could go there now and she could show him what she wanted to take. She stood and watched the men begin packing away the kitchen, plates and food supplies. Her hands had been shaking as she put the few personal items like photographs and books inside the box that Mars held out for her. He was telling her about how when the Institute's new premises were built, everything that was here would be moved there and her apartment would be even better, she would be part of a buzzing environment with other families as well as offices, laboratories and conference centres.

He led her up to her new apartment, passing her the key once he unlocked the door, showed her around and then he left. By the end of the day, she knew she needed to leave and get as far away from him as possible. She was just an insignificant piece on the board of this game he was playing. Her wishes, her choices were irrelevant, and would always be. She began her own secretive manoeuvres, finding a place to live and moving into it. Then severing all contact with him, except through another lawyer, not the one that was helping her with understanding Sebastian's estate but a different one. All contact with Mars would be via that office. She could very well envisage Mars's rage once he discovered her gone. She would've preferred to leave the country but her late term pregnancy precluded that, she would do that once her baby arrived.

She took a break, and lay down on her bed, lying sideways with the body pillow providing some extra support. From this position she was able to look out though the windows at the mauve lotus flowers that had opened up in the sunshine. Dragonflies, scarlet red and golden-brown were darting among the leaves and flowers. She felt the foxes around her, one was guarding the door, another was sitting at the foot of her bed and the flame vixen was outstretched on the bed, her green eyes, like the spring leaves of a gingko stared at her.

"Mother," Takara whispered, as she fell asleep.

Chapter Twenty-three

I will not hesitate to cast upon you the shadow
thrown by the darkness of human life.
But do not be afraid.
Gaze steadfastly into this darkness, and find there the things that
will be of use to you.

Natsume Sōseki

The Present – Japan

Riku had gone to the island; she always felt like an intruder, that somehow, she didn't belong here, but it was here she felt particularly close to her brother. Here she felt his presence, and she needed that right now. She needed to do something, and she needed to feel there was support, his support, even if his support came from the other side.

She sat on one of the stone benches that were placed amid the herb garden; the plants were flourishing, everything was rampantly luxurious; it really was an oasis. The island and its buildings were discreetly hired out to corporations for week-long conferences, the payments helping with the maintenance and upkeep of the property.

Thirty-three years, she thought to herself, thirty-three years since Namiyo and Maeve had disappeared, never to be seen again. Sixteen years since her beloved niece had been brutally murdered and her baby taken somewhere; lost as if she had died, and yet now the child had been found. Riku couldn't believe it, and yet the report was very detailed and even included some photos. The fact that Takara's daughter was now living at the institute, directly under Mars's control filled her with dread.

That monster, she could envisage his face quite clearly, she remembered the funeral, he was disgusting in his arrogance and his fake sadness; it wasn't even sadness, more an annoyance that he had been thwarted. Her mother had never recovered from that event and she had suffered a stroke a few days after the news; only her iron determination to find the child had kept her alive this long. Yet she was now very frail, Riku could see that, only her dark eyes blazed in that sunken face.

"We must bring the child back," she had whispered. "We cannot allow her to remain with him. We cannot. We must do whatever it takes. We are her family, her blood family. Find a way, Riku. Find a way."

Riku knew she was right, but how. The lawyers that they had employed all those years ago, that had hired private detectives in the beginning to look into Takara's death. Even when one of their detectives had been found floating in the harbour, half gnawed by sharks, they had kept the investigation going – although more discreetly, finding out what information they could, paying people inside the police force to relay anything that came their way. It was the adult son of the original lawyer who was now her main contact. Each day he emailed something to her about this young woman called Raven. Something he had found out about her past, where she had been, people who knew her. He was putting together a case and DNA from Namiyo and Maeve had been sent to him, and the laboratories had confirmed a match.

Riku knew that as blood relatives they had more right than that evil psychopath had, to be her guardian. "Namiyo what do we do?" she whispered. "How do we bring her home? We need help. We are relying on legal ways and yet they can bind us for years. We need something, someone more on the ground. We need an ally."

She closed her eyes, felt the gentle breeze caress her face, she could smell the salt in the air, and the herbs, their aromas wafting around her, warmed in the sunshine, their oils drifting as scent molecules in the air. She remembered when Maeve had begun planting the garden; it was really early on before she had married Namiyo even. Riku had come over for a few days and had ended up working with Maeve, helping her plant some of the seedlings and then watering them in the late afternoon sunshine. She had wondered if any of the plants would survive; the soil seemed lacking in nutrients, it seemed so arid and harsh and yet look at them, they were strong and hardy and resilient. They still flourished.

She smiled at the memory and opened her eyes. She was looking at the citrus grove that had been planted as a circular wall around the herbs, the trees were just coming into blossom, she could see the buds beginning to form within the green glossy leaves. Soon they would open up and the scent of their perfume would be even more overpowering; it would perfume the air and the days would be full of the sound of the bees buzzing, while birds and butterflies fluttered around. She felt tears gather in her eyes. It was so sad that none of them were here, her beloved brother and

Maeve should be here, and Takara should be here, sitting with her beautiful daughter, laughing together in the sunshine. Aoi should be here too, living out her final days being nurtured by her family, watching them and smiling as they gathered around her.

***

She sighed as she wiped her eyes, and the memory came to her. Maeve standing beside one of the citrus trees, it was smaller than the others, spindlier and a bit gnarled and crooked. "I'm not sure about this one," Maeve had said. "It's not thriving like the others, no matter what I do, it just doesn't seem to grow properly." And then Maeve had begun crying. "It reminds me of my son, he never seemed as strong and healthy as all the other children."

And that was when Riku had first heard about Maeve's son.

She stood up. Of course, the son, Takara's brother, he had been the detective involved on the original case. He had pursued Mars with a vengeance, even getting himself suspended at one point for his dogged determination that Mars was behind the botched caesarean, as it was called. He hadn't called it that; he had called it manslaughter and possibly murder. The transcripts of his reports were coming back to her. Her lawyer had confirmed that the detective was indeed Maeve's son. Did he know that Takara was his sister? There was something about his refusal to give up on the case that made her think he might know who Takara had been. And he was still there, that was obvious in the recent reports.

She laughed, "thank you, Namiyo. Thank you, Maeve. Yes, we have our ally."

She walked around the citrus grove and came to that tree. It had survived and thrived, not quite as the others, it was more gnarled and misshapen than them, it had a presence and she recalled that the fruit that grew on it was more juicy and tastier.

"I should've done it earlier," she said to the tree. "I had the letters that Maeve had written him, and that his father had sent back unopened. I'd always thought to find a way to send them to him. It's been too long but I can do it now. I can send him those as well as the videos Takara made. I'll ask his help, and I just know that he will help us. I can feel it."

Something caught her eye, something on the grass near the base of this tree. She kneeled down and moved away some of the mulch that was wrapped around the tree trunk. Her fingers curled around the small statue, it was a plastic toy fox, she lifted it up and brushed away the dry stalks.

"Thank you," she said as she bowed. "Thank you, and with the Kitsune with us, we have indeed some powerful allies."

Chapter Twenty-four

And after a while she had a little daughter as white as snow,
as red as blood and with hair as black as ebony.
And when the child was born the queen died.

Brothers Grimm

The door opened, he took off his shades and smiled his wonderful smile. She felt herself fall; her heart plummeted and a chilly wintry wind blew through her and made her shiver. He reached over and stroked her face; very tenderly, very gently. He kissed her lightly on the mouth and whispered to her in a language she almost didn't understand, and she felt herself splintering inside. She felt his heartbeat, it seemed to echo with hers, one beat his, and the next beat hers. His arms were warm and his body strong and sturdy. There was a familiar smell that had nothing to do with perfume or man-made fragrance but was the distillation of his body and soul. She breathed it in, wanting to keep it with her forever, so she would always have it as a remembrance. She pulled herself away. If she stayed in his arms any longer, she would succumb, she would be unable to resist, she would have too many regrets.

Something momentous was about to happen, and it had nothing to do with the party that they were attending. Halo could feel energies accumulating around Raven, phantoms and dreams pushing at the boundaries of reality. He felt he was playing a game for which he had no knowledge of the rules. Raven was somehow part of the game itself; she was the queen figure. By her moves would the game be won or lost.

They arrived at the mansion just before four p.m. The house was on the bay; it faced west, and the sun flooded the rooms and outside lawns. They entered through the large stained glass doors. The place was already crowded; Azûrâ and her father were standing together at the base of a huge sweeping staircase and greeted them both. Then Azûrâ took Raven's hand. Feeling trepidation, Halo watched as they walked away.

A woman he recognised as one of Raven's companions, passed him a glass of champagne and asked him how he was. He muttered something, and then walked off, he knew it was rude, but he didn't really care. He scanned the room and saw Jo at the far end. He pushed his way through the crowd and reached her. She leaned over, lightly kissed his cheek and whispered, "that's her over there, wearing that red dress, isn't it?"

He looked where she was pointing, Raven stood with two men, one was Azûrâ's father, the other he assumed because of his height and presence was Mars.

"Yes. Is Connor here?"

"He's outside having a cigarette," she said. "You look worried, is there a reason?"

"Maybe," he replied but didn't elaborate. He saw Azûrâ walk past with one of her musicians, she must be playing soon, he thought, she glanced in his direction but didn't say anything.

He watched Raven; she looked amazing in that dress he thought. Older, more sophisticated somehow, is that what a few weeks in a rich environment does, he wondered. She had a self-assurance and confidence that hadn't been evident before.

Jo didn't say anything; she took his hand and led him outside through what seemed like an endless array of gaudily-dressed people. Connor was standing on a patch of lawn that led to a small, private beach. The placid, calm bay shone golden in the late afternoon sun. Connor, despite his ugliness looked very stylish in his suit.

"Does she know we are here?" he asked.

"No," Halo replied.

***

Raven had walked out onto the verandah; it was a curving wooden type with intricate lattice and ironwork surrounding it. The plants that grew around it were exotic and unusual. A rose bush clambered up one of the balustrades, it was still flowering, the flowers were apricot hued and richly scented. She reached up to touch one; there was someone beside her, he plucked one of the roses and inhaled its scent deeply.

She turned, expecting to see Halo but it was a stranger. He was slightly built with long black hair. His eyes were very dark almost black. He was in his early thirties, she judged, and there was something decadent in his poise. His smile was very sensual. He asked her name. She didn't answer. He picked another one of the rose blooms and placed it in her hair, securing it behind the pearl comb.

"If you won't tell me, I will have to call you by a name that I choose." He appraised her body and her face fully. She blushed.

"I shall call you Lily," he said. "Long and delicate and white with just a hint of darkness. It is the name that suits you."

"Do you sing, my little lily?" he asked. "Do you speak?"

"Only when I have something to say," Raven said.

"Nice voice, quite low and husky. What do you sing?" he asked but didn't wait for an answer. "I have a way of guessing trends. I am rarely wrong. I like your look. It's simple yet feminine. You look fragile but there is something of the punk goddess in you too. Big eyes. Black hair. Luscious lips." He leaned closer and said in conspiratorial whispers, "shall I make you a star my Lily? I could, you know. I could make you famous." His eyebrows lifted and he laughed. "My name is Hartley by the way."

"How can you be sure? You haven't heard me sing. I could be awful," she asked calmly.

"You'd be surprised how many singers start off with terrible voices. Singing is one part practice, one part talent, and two parts being in the right place at the right time. It has less to do with the voice and more to do with the ability of the person to convey complex, tangled emotions. Singing is the touching of the soul. It is the soaring above the earth. It is like fucking an angel." He laughed again.

Raven looked away from his face and out over the lawns, the well-kept shrubs and down to the water's edge, which was shining like molten gold.

"Tell me your thoughts, Lily," Hartley said.

Raven was silent.

"Come and see me next week. Here's my contact."

She looked at the wafer; it was black parchment with a spinning logo and his name, El Diablo.

She looked at him, he had become a devil, red eyes and skin-like black leather, as he laughed, he turned to flame. She dropped the wafer, which self-combusted in a puff of red smoke, and backed into Halo who was standing behind her.

"Raven," he said. "There are some people I would like you to meet."

She turned and looked at the two people waiting. She looked into the eyes of an extremely ugly man, well dressed and older. She didn't know him, yet there was something very familiar about him. Her hand reached for the pendant involuntarily, she knew who he was.

"I'm sorry if my presence here alarms you," Connor said gently. "I thought we might have a moment to talk, if you care to."

She nodded but before she could say anything she felt a pressure on her arm. She looked up to see Mars standing next to her.

"You do turn up in the most unlikely of places," Mars drawled. He was staring at Connor. "I don't recall inviting you." He looked at all of them his eyes disdainful, before saying. "Detective, please don't make me find an excuse to have you thrown out." There was a smirk of annoyance on his face and although he was a very handsome man, his face looked far more unpleasant than the detective's.

"Raven, I have some other, more appropriate people I'd like you to meet." He took her by the arm and led her away.

"I think we just lost our opportunity," Connor said.

Halo watched her depart and inside he felt even edgier than he had before. He could hear music; he recognised Azûrâ's voice singing. He felt caught between two worlds and it would be so easy to let all this go; Raven, the slipstream,

Connor and Jo, go back to his previous life, hitch up with Azûrâ again. There was a feeling of nostalgia as he thought back; it had all been too easy, just fun, drugs to get you higher than a rocket and gorgeous girls that were happy to indulge in whatever was on offer. No strings. No messy emotions. What the fuck had changed? Why did I get involved in all of this? When did all this become my problem?

He looked at Jo. She looked like she knew exactly what he was thinking. He walked away and picked up a glass of champagne and drank it as he scanned the crowd. Two pretty girls dressed in identical costumes, black almost see through sheaths smiled at him. He walked over and began talking to them.

"Give him some time," Connor said to Jo. "We haven't lost him, he just needs to remember what's important."

***

Twenty minutes later he found himself in one of the bathrooms, all mirrored surfaces and shiny steel. "This is wicked shit," one of the girls said as she lined up some black crystals along the mirrored surface. The black crystals sucked in the light; they looked ominous, like tiny black holes on the stainless steel. They reminded him of the slipstream. Halo dipped his little finger and had a taste, bitter and numbing, he felt a small buzz almost immediately.

The other girl draped herself over him and began kissing him; her breath was acrid and he wondered how many lines she had already done. The pupils in her eyes were so dilated he couldn't even tell what colour her eyes were. She was naked under her dress, through the sheer fabric it was almost like he was touching her skin. Her face was beautiful, but somehow vacant, like a doll. How much of her was real, he wondered. Her face, her body, how much was plastic? She pushed him back against the wall, and he looked up at a mirrored ceiling where the three of them were reflected back, he noticed that even the floor was mirrored. He felt the girl's hand slide between his thighs, and he pushed her away gently.

"Just realised that I have to be somewhere now."

"What?" both girls said at once. "We can't have all of this ourselves."

"I'm sure you'll find some very grateful dudes to share this with," Halo replied as he reached for the door and squeezed himself out through the narrow opening. He had no idea where he was in the vast house but headed where the music was loudest.

***

In a moment of iciness, the figure appeared before Raven, and she was looking into his eyes of shadowed violet. His face was pale; the skin stretched tightly over his cheekbones, his hair was short and the blondeness of a pure white dove.

"Ceriful," she whispered.

"I've come to say goodbye," he said in a voice that seemed to encompass all the sadness in the world.

"No!" she cried.

"Yes. The sun will soon set, and I must depart as the moon rises. I have an hour – maybe a little longer." His voice was strained, and she sensed the effort it cost him to be here. Her heart fluttered in her chest, against her ribs.

"I sense you have made your decision," he whispered again. He reached for her hand and held it in his cold one.

"It keeps changing."

She stared at the dagger of black crystal hanging around his neck and knew that it was frozen distillation of his power. She brushed over it with her fingertips. It was as cold as a comet and as blazing. Silver stars seemed to swirl within it.

"There is still time," he said with such longing that tears filled her eyes.

Halo walked into the large room and saw Raven, she was talking intensely to someone, his white-blonde hair was familiar, he turned his head slightly and Halo saw his profile. He saw the stranger from his dream. That face. He was here. This was it. The game stood in harsh focus. It was nearing completion. Only a few moves left. He looked at Raven. She stood enthralled. She knew him that was obvious. Everything he had feared was happening.

Halo began walking towards her through the crowd; his glance took in the mirror which hung above the marble fireplace which reflected the room and all those in it. Except one.

His gaze returned to that face, those weird eyes that were now riveted on Raven. He was here, and he was way more dangerous than Mars.

"You have no idea how badly you've fucked up."

The voice next to him made him turn. Azûrâ was glaring at him.

"I can see you are about to enlighten me," he said wryly.

"You really don't know how powerful half these people in this room are. You could've gone so far. You had the opportunity of a lifetime, and you choose the wrong side."

"I don't think I did, Azûrâ. I think I made the right decision."

She looked surprised as though she hadn't expected that response, then she laughed. "You are such a cowboy, aren't you? Think you can stay on the outer and not get dragged into the real world. Just hang with that underclass that you find so appealing. There is no real power there."

"Wouldn't be too sure of that."

"You're not as hot as you think you are," she snarled.

"Neither are you, sweetheart." He replied. He looked around the room; Raven and the stranger were gone.

He headed towards the front door, jostling his way through the crowd. He hurried down the steps and looked over at the vast driveway. He saw her black limousine pull out and glide its way down towards the huge gates.

Jo reached his side. "What's happened?"

"Raven has gone."

"Where?" Connor hurried down the stairs after them.

Halo thought for a moment. "I think I know where she might be going."

"Well, come on then, I've got a fast car; let's see if we can find her," Jo said.

She was right about the fast car – it looked like something that should be in a museum, but it really moved. "My grandfather was a racing driver, and this is one of his, which I have lovingly restored," she said as they weaved in and out of the traffic. "So, where am I going?"

"We need to head towards the Westside checkpoint. There's an old, abandoned area we call the Ghostlands."

"I know the place," Connor said. "The old Western quarantine sector. It's where we found the dead man with a strand of her hair in his hand. Why does she go there?"

"She told me once that it's the only place where she can't hear the endless noise of our world. The electromagnetic resonance sometimes overwhelms her. It's quiet there. Phones don't work; there are no communication towers. She told me she goes there to get away from it all."

"She's very sensitive, isn't she?" Jo commented. "This world must seem like an absolute madhouse to her."

"You said quarantine sector. What was there previously?" Halo asked.

"Did they teach you about the Plague years?" Connor said.

"They brushed over it," Halo replied.

"Thirty years ago, when the New Plague came through, that area was a well-to-do suburb, high-density housing but affluent. The first cases were reported there, and they quarantined part of it. As more cases appeared, the quarantine area grew until it took up that entire western sector. So, the government decided to close it all off. There was no cure and the real risk of it spreading, so they built high voltage fencing and shot anyone who attempted to leave. They kept the electricity and water going in but cut off communications. They didn't want people on the outside being able to see or hear what was happening. They thought it might lead to a revolution. So, they blacked out all communication, there were buffers and shields set up along the perimeter and the place was effectively sealed off. That's probably why she can't hear the noise. Some of those buffers and shields are no doubt still working."

He was silent, and when he spoke there was such sadness in his voice. "They burned the dead. Sometimes the fires spread into the buildings and took hold, burning for days. The whole horizon would be red with fire. The sunsets were quite spectacular. They say it took nearly ten years for the last of the residents to die. That's what they say but no one really knows. I was much younger – in my early teens when it began, and I used to think about all those souls locked away, given the bare essentials but knowing that there was no hope. The inhumanity of what we do to each other."

Connor looked out the window, a few minutes later, he said. "Turn off here. They are redeveloping the site now, and it's been judged safe, but many of the old roads are demolished, so we will need to go carefully."

When they got there, the entire area was ablaze with arc lights and it almost looked like day; the bulldozers and trucks crushing their way through the buildings. With the rubble piling up, the place looked like a war zone. The road ended in a mass of upended concrete. Jo pulled the car over and they climbed out.

They began walking. Halo felt he was walking through a graveyard and the feeling made him sway with foreboding. He called her name, but the noise from the trucks was a constant hum that blotted out other sounds. It was a clear night, cooling fast after the warm day. He found the flower that he remembered seeing in her hair; he had almost crushed it, he picked it up tenderly, and it emitted a sweet fragrance. He felt a sense of doom, a remembrance of carrying a crushed flower in the palm of his hand before, a death – a preventable death, the petals darkening like dry blood. He thrust the flower into the pocket of his vest.

Halo sat down on a piece of rusted girder; they would never be able to search all the buildings and their only hope was to somehow pinpoint where she was. His mind raced through that dream and the ensuing conversation with the stranger. Was the stranger a manifestation of some dark part of himself? Was it real? What was real, anyway?

Then in a moment of intense lucidity, the mirror flashed across his mind.

To see in a mirror, one needs light.

Mirror.

Dark.

Reflection.

Blood.
Moon.
Possession.
Desire.
Death.
The words entangled in his mind, bringing up random images like a search engine gone into hyperdrive. Breathe, he told himself. Halo felt an unearthly tug, as though his blood was ebbing and flowing through his veins like a strange red ocean. The full moon loomed monstrous, visible now above the horizon, and the loonies, the predators, and those blessed with gypsy visions, and some of the children and all the moths sensed the coming of the sun's mirror.

***

Raven and Ceriful stood together on the dusty floorboards. The air had become translucent and misty, and fluttered like lacy curtains in an evening breeze. Above their heads, the sky was visible, comets swarmed, and stars seemed to fall like snowflakes. Ceriful stood with his arms around Raven, her red dress fluttered against his dark garments. From his back, wings began to grow; feather-like, ivory. They reached full size, and the colour changed or maybe it just drained away. The wings had become black, like ink or oil or night. His wings beat slowly, languidly.

For one brief moment she thought of Halo and her heart fluttered with regret and Ceriful almost lost his hold. Halo felt her near and he began to run towards the derelict warehouse calling her name. Jo and Connor followed, they rounded a corner and suddenly they were in what seemed to be a vortex of light and dark. It was the slipstream huge and seemingly never-ending. Galaxies spun above them, stars fell, suns were born and died, and the entire spectrum of colour swirled around them like a tide sweeping in and out. At the periphery of their vision, spectres and phantoms danced and cavorted. It was like nothing they had ever seen before.

"How much energy is this taking?" Halo asked awed by the immensity of it. "The cost of holding this here must be enormous."

"Seven cities have fallen off the grid so far to make this work, there may be more. There will be a huge headache tomorrow for those who have to try and explain what happened," the voice said gleefully.

"Why?" he asked the angel.

"I needed to anchor this here in your world temporarily. It's a bridge. Too many leakages have occurred; I need to bring my pets home. I need a pathway for my Queen."

"You're not even real," Halo said. "An illusion. A construct. Electricity and code encased somewhere on a circuit board. Have you told her what you really are?"

"How is that different from you? Electromagnetic energy running with instructions imparted by Deoxyribonucleic acid and encased in meat. Are we really that different you and I?" He asked and then laughed. "She understands better than you. She has made her choice."

Halo said softly, ever so softly, "stay."

Raven looked into his eyes, so blue like the sky at twilight, she wavered momentarily and then looked up at Ceriful, closed her eyes and listened to the gentle swishing of his wings.

"I have to do this, Halo," Raven said. "I know you don't understand, but trust me."

"He lies. He plays with us. You know what he is; he is the spider that sits in the middle of this web. He is a supreme predator, he doesn't even hunt us, he just seduces us with his stories. So perfectly attuned to what we are; they resonate so profoundly that we can't help but become enthralled. What was he when he first came? Something innocent, I'm guessing like a unicorn?"

Her eyes stared into his, confirming his reasoning.

"I'm right aren't I?" he continued. "And now he is an Angel. Almost human but more alluring, not as frightening as a God, and certainly nowhere near as carnal as if he came as a man, or as frightening if he showed his true capabilities and came as the monster he really is. He has found what most appeals to you and is using that to ensnare you."

"You are really so much like me," Ceriful interrupted him. "I am no different to you; you recognise the seduction because it is what you do. I just have more tools at my disposal, that is all. But fundamentally what I offer is real. Raven understands that. You cannot compete with what is on offer here."

"So, what is it that you so desperately need from her?" Halo asked.

"I do like your quick grasp of things. What would a creature like me want with her? What is it that I could possibly need? Desire? A soul perhaps, isn't that what the dark always craves from the light?" Ceriful laughed as his black wings languidly beat the air. "I'll leave you with that little question to ponder."

"Halo. Remember and understand," Raven said. "Know that I have made this choice." Her voice was so soft and gentle.

"This is for you Halo," Ceriful said softly. "A special show. Do watch and enjoy."

Halo watched as Ceriful tilted Raven's head forward and brushed aside the tendrils of black hair. Watched as he stroked her neck so white, so smooth and took the black shining crystal dagger from around his neck and cut two long slashes from the base of her neck, curving around the shoulder blades. Blood dripped down her back framed by her black hair.

Red. White. Black.

As black as ebony.

As white as snow.

As red as blood.

Fairytales often contain the essence of life, of truth within their words.

Night.

Moon.

Blood.

The essence that was Raven flowed into the slipstream; it was sweet like a rose with the dew still sparkling on it, fragile like a lark's song, ephemeral as a rainbow, strong as a spider-web. As her essence emptied, Raven began her own transformation as what was called flowed back into her. The wings that bloomed from her skin were crimson like a monstrous ruby, the feathers of a firebird, the beginning of a power reborn.

For there is always an equal return; what is taken, is given.

Music swelled within the slipstream; the song of the cosmos flowed around them, the universe vibrated like a choir of infinite violins, darkness and light slithered between them like rainbow serpents. Then, as from far away, a bell tolled, mysterious and compelling, something from the ship of an ancient mariner.

And the world fell away and became nothing.

The mirror cracked from side to side.

The moon rose.

And faraway yet ever so close.

Falling.
Falling.
Falling.
Spinning.
Burning.
Falling.

A match fell a long, long way, spinning and burning and enjoying its hot transient moment and, just as it had almost reached the end of its fuel and it was feeble and tiny; it met up with a host of gaseous ghosts and it flared once more. Its energy collided with the ether and a miniature sun, for the briefest of moments, shone underground.

The blast reverberated within those forgotten caverns, and a low rumbling grew into an enormous thunder, like the deadly approach of a runaway train about to reach maximum velocity and destruction. It blew the buildings apart in a blaze of fire and heat that lit up the surrounding area as though it were day. It rippled through the underground networks of pipes and antechambers, it made a crater the size of a small meteorite. It ripped apart the electricity cables and the arc lights went dead. The dozers and the trucks stopped work, confused.

Across town, a chandelier tinkled perceptibly but it was doubtful that anyone noticed, except Azûrâ who looked up at the diamond cut glass that was still trembling, and felt the same trembling go through her body.

The moon rose high in the sky, a yellow harvest moon depicting the turning of the seasons, the turning of the tides, the turning of a moment. The answer came to Halo as he lay dazed on the ground, and his last thoughts before he blacked out were of her, her hair as black as ebony, her skin as white as snow, her wings as red as blood.

The mirror shattered.

Chapter Twenty-five

All the chrysanthemums that there are; lay them in the coffin.

Natsume Sōseki

The address that he had been given was for one of the most desirous restaurants in the city; a place so exclusive that the address was not known. He knocked on the red door with the black number 333 etched onto a plaque on the rough slate wall.

He gave his name to the suited man who answered, and was led down a long corridor and then up a flight of stairs to an open space with some comfortable couches arranged against a wall. He was told to sit, and a young woman came with a tray that held a glass of iced water and a teapot cup combo. He lifted the lid, lemongrass and ginger aromas floated up into the air. He put the lid back on and waited. A few minutes later, a young man came and asked Connor to follow him. Opening a door into a large sized room that was ornately but simply decorated, he walked down the slim stairs to the sunken dining area and sat on one of the covered benches that surrounded the long table.

He looked around his surroundings; discreet skylights with opaque rice paper screens provided the diffused light along with covered lanterns in corner alcoves. A small-cultivated indoor garden took up one wall, miniature black stalked bamboo provided the backdrop and in the foreground was a small, pebbled pond with orange and pink koi swishing through the water. Other plants – and what looked like large bonsai – grew between the artfully placed jagged rocks, a skylight with louvres allowed rays of sunshine to pour over the pond, the plants, and the raked sand.

Connor decided that regardless of the identity of the mystery person who was behind this clandestine meeting, he might as well enjoy himself. He was unlikely to ever come here again, regardless of what repercussions this all might bring.

A few minutes later, he lifted his head to see the door open and a young man in a suit walk down the steps and take up the seat across from him. The briefcase that he carried he placed next to him.

"Thank you for coming, Connor O'Hara, I appreciate that you have."

The man was probably in his twenties; Asian, most likely Japanese, considering where they were meeting.

"Your name?" Connor asked.

The man smiled. "You can call me Justin if you need a name. I am merely a messenger, an emissary of the family that wish to begin a dialogue with you. This room has been booked for two hours, and a selection of dishes has already been prepared for you. Soon, a waiter will come to see what drinks you want. Please, order anything."

He lifted the case, placed it on the table and opened it. He pulled out a laptop and pushed it across the table. "This is for you, it is brand new, and it has contact details of the woman who wishes to talk with you. It has my contact details as well if you need to get in touch."

He pulled out a carefully folded paper from his pocket and passed it over as well. "These are the three passwords you will need to login, please change them within three days."

Connor stared at the laptop, making no move towards it or the folded up paper. He looked at the man across him, who stared back with a slight smile. The man reached inside the case and pulled out an envelope. He pushed that across the table.

"This will answer most of your questions," he said. "Everything else within this case is for you, some of it is of a personal nature. Mr. O Hara – and I deliberately call you that – you are our guest as a private citizen, not as an officer of the law. I understand that it can be hard to separate the personal from the professional, but in this case I hope you understand that the reasons for this invitation have more to do with you being the brother of Takara Takenaka, than anything else. Of course the fact you worked on her murder case all those years ago, and also recently with the reappearance of her daughter Raven, cannot always be separated. Please know that the family that wish to open up communication with you are sincere in this and would not want to compromise you in anyway."

Justin – or whatever his actual name was – had a steady gaze, Connor thought, which in itself was unusual as there was no intimidation or any other bullshit there, the man either had an excellent poker face, or was genuine.

"As I said, you are a guest, plates of food will arrive, eat whatever you want, order whatever you please, this room is yours for two hours, but if you want to stay longer, you may." He paused. "If you choose to not take the laptop, you may leave it here. You may leave right now if you choose, although I do hope that you at least read the letter. The woman who has written to you, is very genuine and sincere; her main concern is the welfare of Raven. Takara was like her daughter; she raised her after her parents died, the death and the disappearance of her baby have haunted her these past sixteen years."

He stood up, "I take my leave, I'm at your disposal if you choose to remain in contact. Please know that this place is very discreet, no one will ever know you were here. The rooms are shielded from all manner of scanners, security is probably way tighter than your offices. No one is listening, no one is watching." He bowed slightly, then left.

Connor sat staring at the envelope for what felt like a long time but was probably only a few minutes. The woman, who had brought him the water and tea earlier, appeared again with another tray of iced water, and a teapot and a cup this time. She placed these on the table and presented him with a drinks menu that was on silky parchment covered with amazing calligraphy. He ordered an aged whisky and a small jug of sake.

Before going, she poured him a cup of the tea, the aroma was delicately fragrant, and he lifted the cup and took a sip. It was delicious he had to admit. He asked her if there was any place he could go to have a cigarette. She giggled.

"Come," she said as she led him over to the garden, she pressed a button and a portion of the wall moved. Behind the tall bamboos was a space with two reclining chairs and a small side table. "Please use whenever, there is a fan that removes smoke and filters the air."

He returned with his cup and the envelope. The chair was quite possibly the most comfortable chair that he had ever sat in. He lit a cigarette and opened the envelope.

It was a long letter. His whisky arrived, and he read the letter again as he drank it.

He stayed. It was personal; he could see that, regardless of his professional involvement, which he knew would be an underlying factor in why they had contacted him. The welfare of Raven, was at the heart of this. As well as justice for her mother. Although they didn't wish to compromise him, it was inevitable; he knew the system too well to not understand that no matter how well intentioned they were, if the powers above got a whiff of this, he would be severely compromised – even if he passed on only what was reported in the public media.

He also knew that justice was not always served; the rich and powerful still got away with more than the less privileged, and if this involved anyone else apart from his sister and her daughter, he would've walked out. But his sister's murder still haunted him, and Raven's well-being was still his concern. He found Riku's comment; that no matter how strange and unbelievable the circumstances of Raven's disappearance may be; Riku wanted him to know she was open to all possibilities. He felt instinctively that she might be the one person that he would be able to tell what had occurred that night – he owed her that regardless of whether she would believe what he saw.

The food arrived at intervals; he ate as he read through the documents she had sent. He left the bundle of his mother's letters and Takara's videos for when he was home; he wasn't sure how he would react to those, but what he did find within the information he had read was many of the missing pieces that had gnawed away at him for years. Suddenly he could see the picture so much clearer. And it was stranger than he had envisaged. As the last dish was taken away and a black espresso was scenting the air with its rich aroma, he finally realised that he needed Riku as much as she needed him.

He also knew that if he had the choice of staying in the force and dropping these two cases – which at any time was a quite likely scenario – he knew he would choose to leave and continue his pursuit as a freelancer. And if he did, he would need the resources that Riku would be able to provide. He packed everything away and asked the same young woman who had come to clear away the final plates, if she would show him out.

She giggled again as she led him out of the room into the hallway and along another hallway, down stairs to another level, and then into an elevator which was so smooth he couldn't work out if they were going down or up. When the door opened, there were more hallways and stairs, and then into a room which contained a table and chairs.

"Someone will be here in a moment. Domo arigato," she bowed, her face serious even as she giggled.

She left, and as the door closed, he could not see where it had been; it was just part of the wall. Another door opened. An older man escorted him out and then through a large and very busy sushi restaurant, to the front door.

Out on the street, Connor could see he was now in a totally different part of the city – a more familiar part of the city – and he decided it was best he not think too much about where he had been, and who was behind that establishment; not the celebrity owners that were occasionally in the social news, but the money and power behind them.

But he had to admit that it was probably the best meal he had ever eaten.

Chapter Twenty-six

"The lamps are different, but the Light is the same.
One matter, one energy,
one Light….

Rumi

The city skyline and the pallid night were alive with glowing pumpkins, melting ghosts, sexy witches on broomsticks, and skin-shedding zombies. Tonight was Halloween, All Hallows' Eve, Samhain, the Celtic festival of the Dead – the night when the spirits could pass from their world to ours. Halo sat on the rooftop with Jo and the Gargoyle. They were sharing some cocktails and watching the show.

"My suspension is now over," Connor said. "I need a suspension every now and again; it's the closest I get to a holiday." He smiled at them both.

He didn't quite look as ugly when he smiled, Halo thought, or maybe he was just getting used to the man.

"Any other repercussions?" Jo asked.

"Mars couldn't do much really. After all she was his ward and she left in the limousine he had provided her. He had to face up to some questioning on his responsibilities,"

Connor looked over at Halo. "He was one furious dude. And getting me suspended for crashing his party was just his way of reminding me he could do what the fuck he wanted to me. I submitted a report regardless and made the obvious comment about who benefits from her disappearance. He does if she is not around; he owns one hundred percent of the company. If she is alive, they share equally. So, who has the motive? It's first year detective work. I made sure that some of that was leaked out to the press. I don't imagine he liked some of the articles that came out about that."

"I can imagine he would be more pissed," Halo said. He took a sip of his drink; it was spicy with a hint of chilli.

"Jo," Halo said, "you mentioned you have found out something."

"I have," she smiled. "I got close to one of the researchers working at the institute. I met him at that party, he was a little bewitched by me." She laughed before continuing. "So, that made him careless as he tried to impress me with all the wonderful things he could do. I managed to use his credentials to have a bit of a look around in their super secure systems. Unfortunately, I may have gotten the young man terminated, job wise; he still breathes. I found some information about Raven, because Mars originally used a rather sentimental reason on why he wanted the baby, which never rang true with me. The man is as cold blooded as they come. 'The baby's only importance is its genetic make-up' are the words you said he used." Jo looked over at Connor.

"Raven has inherited what sounds like the remote viewing skills of her mother, but she has way more than that; she had obviously inherited from her father as well. Brilliant as he was, it was less obviously defined what had come down via him. Sebastian was a geneticist and he played around with his DNA. There are secret files. Sorry I couldn't get them, but I read enough to grasp that he had managed to do what many have thought impossible, he had manipulated his DNA to some extent and it seems he had manipulated Raven's DNA in utero. I think that is the key to why Mars so wanted her and was prepared to go to such extremes to have her. What her father did and what that means is open to all sorts of possibilities, but…" she looked over at Halo, "that may also be why she is so crucial to the Slipstream Spider – or whatever-he-is."

Halo let that sink in for a few moments. He accepted a cigarette from Connor and blew the smoke out in small perfect smoke rings that floated up into the sky, drifting between a skeleton and a flock of red-eyed bats.

"But we don't know exactly what he did to himself or her."

Jo shook her head. "Now what have you found out?" she asked.

Halo laughed, how she seemed to read his mind left him always slightly off balance.

"I've found a way into the slipstream; it's very small, very hard to find, but it's a way in." he finally said.

"So let me guess. You're planning a trip in?" Connor said.

Halo nodded, he could feel a lecture coming his way. "I know what I'm doing," he said defensively.

"Really," Jo said. "You really think you are on top of this? All alone against that entity." She looked over at Connor. "The impetuous and recklessness of youth! Was I ever like this?"

Connor laughed. "You really aren't expecting me to answer that are you?"

Jo said to Halo, "No. We go in together. And we're going to spend some time honing the skills we need. You are going to show me this back door, and then we can ascertain whether it's a trap or not. Do not underestimate the danger we will face in there. He brought down ten cities, blacked them out for twelve hours just to create his pathway and put on that show. Thousands of people died from their emergency meds being off-line. Not to mention the other deaths and the chaos that almost brought down two governments. The military alliances are still trying to work out what happened and meanwhile have used this as an excuse to invade one of the regimes they don't like. We have another war looming on the radar. And we have no idea of what he is capable of. And with Raven, what he has access to now. Let alone what his plans are."

"I thought you'd say something like that," Halo said.

"Also, we have to have somewhere to house these bodies, to make sure they are nourished and kept alive. We have no idea how long we could end up in that virtual space. We've got to come back at some point," she pointed out.

"I know that," he replied.

"I think I can sort that," Connor said quietly. "I'll be able to get what we need. And I'll be there; I'll keep you both safe."

A look passed between Jo and Connor, she knew where he'd get the resources he needed. She smiled at him. *Healing,* she thought, *it's what he needs; he doesn't realise that, but I see the difference, since he received those letters.*

Jo looked at Halo; he was staring up at the buildings, but she sensed he wasn't seeing that – he was somewhere else entirely.

"You've seen her, haven't you?" Jo asked quietly.

"How do you do that?" he replied as he looked at her.

"Sixth sense," she said, but her eyes were compassionate. "So, spill."

"She was here, or here and not here. Some in-between place. I was walking, and I turned a corner and then I was in a garden. It was a frozen garden full of snow and she was there."

He remembered that moment so clearly, as he stood there looking at the trees and bushes submerged by water frozen to this incredible coldness; the light through the open doors shone on the whiteness and it reflected back like a luminous mirror. He could smell pine and juniper in the icy air. He hurried onto the verandah where long icicles hung down, crystalline stalactites and then into the room, with the wooden floors, the panelled ceiling, and the walls made from translucent rice paper screens. He'd been here before. Lanterns wavered from the ceiling and seemed to give out a rich, opulent fragrance. This time, it was she who sat on the floor at the low table; a cape of smoky white fur covering her, and her hair was longer and blacker than he remembered.

Halo leaned over and kissed her with such intensity and longing it left him breathless and caused the icicles to start dripping.

"It usually works in fairy stories," he said to her.

"Who said it didn't work?" Raven whispered and laughed, and in the garden the snow began to melt incredibly slowly – almost imperceptibly – molecule by molecule.

Then she began dissolving; the room and the garden and everything melted away, he as well; melting into rainwater that fell from the skies, soaking the ground, the earth, the soil and creating life. And as he dissolved and became part of the earth, he heard her voice.

"Bring me home," she whispered in the soft muted tones of the rain. "Find me and bring me back."

He had woken to find himself lying in the gutter with the rain falling on him, and the taste of her in his mouth, on his tongue, running through his bloodstream like a strange virus; nestling there, curled up was a tiny glimmering essence sleeping inside him, waiting to reawaken when the time was right. A secret and a key, a pivotal element that now dwelled within him, hidden, waiting like a tiny time bomb.

***

To be continued…

Thank you for reading SLIPSTREAM.
We hope you enjoyed it.

If you would like to be kept informed of further
releases by Alice Godwin, or other new books from
Hague Publishing, why not subscribe to our newsletter at
www.HaguePublishing.com/subscribe.php

And if you loved the book and have a moment to spare
we would really appreciate a short review. Your help in
spreading the word is always gratefully received.

About the Author

Raised in the most southern of Australian cities, Hobart (Nipaluna), capital of the heart-shaped island of Tasmania (Lutruwita), gateway to the Southern Ocean and Antarctica. Impacted by the mystical land of her childhood, Alice can recall days of climbing through Eden-like forests and around glacial waterfalls, where mystical ravens and colorful parrots flew through the Antarctic Beech forests, adding to her sense of wonder in the world around her.

Her family were European exiles from various countries from Turkey to Lithuania. She is the first mother in four generations to give birth to her children in the same country she was born in. Her first job was in the Editorial Library of The Mercury newspaper in Hobart before joining the chaotic, colourful world of fashion in a design studio off Chapel Street in South Yarra, Melbourne. Eventually she headed further north to Sydney and some interesting years working at the Museum of Contemporary Art situated between the iconic Harbour Bridge and the Opera House on Circular Quay.

Around this time she began writing and her first short story was shortlisted in the Northern Territory awards and printed in their anthology 'Extra-Territorial' and so she continued, stopping briefly for a few years when her two sons took her on other adventures. She has had forty short stories published in magazines, anthologies, and literary journals in Australia, USA and UK. She won the Australian Horror Writers Assoc short story of the year (2008), Wyvern Publications UK YA short story competition and has been shortlisted for the Irish Aeon Award.

She is very excited that Hague Publishing is publishing her first novel 'Slipstream' and you can find more about her by visiting her website http://www.alicegodwin.com

Hague

Publishing

www.HaguePublishing.com

PO Box 451 Bassendean
Western Australia 6934